Southern Heat

SPECIAL EDITION

NATASHA MADISON

Southern
heat

Michael nothing and no one can stop you.
I can't wait to see how you change the world.
Just don't forget to come back and visit!

Someday when the pages of my life end,
I know that you will be one of the most beautiful chapters.
Anonymous

Southern Heat
Willow

After being left for dead, I was given a fresh start. I could go anywhere in the world, yet all I wanted was to stay where I was.

Even though I knew I was safe, I always had a bag packed and ready just in case I needed to escape again. As they said, old habits died hard.

Being in the shadows was lonely, but lonely was safe. No one saw me. No one really got to know me.
Except him.

Quinn

Being a cowboy was in my blood, just like my father and his father before him. But unlike my father, the only thing that interested me was my horses.

I was the quiet one, the one who stood in the back and watched things unfold.

Yet the night I found her fighting for her life, something inside me shifted.

I couldn't stop myself from falling in love with her. Even though I knew, in the end, she would leave me.

One

QUINN

I strap on the black bulletproof vest over my black T-shirt. Ethan and Mayson are already dressed and ready to go.

The look on Mayson's face is a mixture of rage and fear as he waits anxiously for the cue to go. It's not every day that your father kidnaps the woman you love.

I put the gun holster on my hip and turn to look over at my father, Casey, and my uncle Jacob as they roll open the house plans.

"The cabin is isolated," my uncle says, and I walk over to see the plan of the forest. "It was a hunting cabin, so it's literally just one room."

"It's time," my cousin Ethan says. "Let's go." He looks over at Mayson, who is one step ahead of him. Mayson and Ethan were in the military together. He showed up here three months ago after being shot and tortured. Chelsea saved him in more ways than he can tell you.

I put on the helmet with the night glasses. "You sure you're okay to go out there?" my father asks as he looks down at the beeping red mark indicating Chelsea's location.

"He's ready," my uncle Jacob says and smirks at me. "I've trained him since he was eight."

"Trained by the best," I say, my whole body tightening with anticipation.

"Okay," my father says. "You two are up."

Jacob and I nod at each other, and I follow his lead. He's been sheriff for this town since before I was born. Walking in the darkness of the forest, we try to be as quiet as we can, but the twigs crack under our boots and branches hit us as we make our way to the cabin.

The sound of my breathing echoes in my ears as my father's voice comes through my headpiece. "Okay, we got eyes on you two. Quinn and Jacob are right behind you."

"We are moving in," Mayson says, and I shake my head.

"Don't be stupid." I press the button to talk. "Wait for backup." But no one answers me. I hear screaming, and Jacob stops in front of me as we look right and left.

"He found the tracker!" my father screams. "Tracker has been found."

"Fuck," I hiss as we sprint toward the cabin. We get there and look at each other as we walk up the three stairs to the front door.

The cabin has seen better days. The wood is almost rotten to the point that if the wind could get around the trees, it would tear it apart.

I walk in right after Jacob and see Ethan standing to the side with his gun drawn. Mayson straddles a man on the floor and punches him, his fists swinging right, then left. It takes me less than a second to see Chelsea lying off to the side with her eyes closed. "Mayson!" I yell his name as Ethan rushes over to him and grabs his wrist in his hand.

"He isn't worth it. You need to go to Chelsea," Ethan says, and he finally gets off the man and walks over to her. My gun is aimed at the man lying in the middle of the dark room.

Mayson says something to her as she moans, and he picks her up. The tears stream down his face, and I have my heart in my throat. She is one of my best friends, and I want to walk out with him, but I know I can't turn my back on this scene.

Mayson turns and walks past his father, coming by Ethan and me as we stand side by side. "Gun!" I hear Jacob yell, and everything happens in slow motion. I turn toward the man on the ground.

He lifts his head as he holds up the black gun in his hand. His face is bloody as he smiles the vilest smile I've ever seen in my life. He aims his gun toward Mayson, who rushes out of the cabin with his head down, covering Chelsea with his body.

"Fuck you," he says to us right before a shot is fired.

"Shots fired!" I yell. The flashing blue and red lights shine into the cabin.

I look over at Jacob, who walks over to Mayson's father, his gun still trained at him. He kicks away the gun from his side as it slides under the lone bed in the room.

"Is he ...?" I look down at the man as he lies there with his eyes open.

Jacob gets down on one knee and picks up his hand, checking for a pulse at his wrist. "No heartbeat."

"How pissed do you think Mayson will be that he didn't pull that trigger?" I look down at the man who has been hunting him for the past three months.

"We have a casualty," Ethan says as he looks down at the man. "Jacob took out Mayson's father."

I look around the room as the light from outside is shining bright. I was not wrong when I said the wind would knock this place down. Light shines in through the cracks around the two windows in the front. I walk over to the fridge, not even attempting to open it. "Try not to touch anything," Jacob says, and I turn to look at the room. The lone table in the middle has a bottle of booze sitting on it. I look over at the door as people enter. A black bag sits in the corner, but no one has noticed it.

"Are you okay?" Ethan looks at me, and I nod.

"Killed or be killed." I repeat what he used to say when he came back from the military. He doesn't really tell me many stories about that time, and to be honest, I'm not one to ask. If he wants to share things with me, he will. If he doesn't, then that's okay, too.

"Did you see that?" I motion with my chin toward the bag. He looks at the bag as we both walk over to it.

"Should you touch that?" he asks as I squat, grabbing the bag. "Well, too late now." I'm reaching to unzip it when something white catches my eye from the side. Two people come in, making a commotion with the stretcher, and Ethan walks to them. Turning my head back around to the side, I stay here glued to the spot as my eyes take in what looks like a shoe right under the bed. Standing, I walk toward the rusty cast-iron bed. The lone mattress on there is covered with yellow stains.

I squat down and tilt my head to peer under it, and the first thing I see is black hair. My heart speeds up even more than it did before. Everything around me is suddenly quiet, or at least that's how it seems to me.

Everything except the beating of my heart can be heard as I push the bed a little, and then I see her long black hair. "Oh my God." I move the bed to see the woman with her face turned away from me. "Ethan!" I shout over my shoulder at him and see him looking back at me.

His eyebrows press together. "I need to move the bed," I say frantically, getting up. Everyone looks over at me, wondering what the hell has gotten into me. I lift the bed and flip it over on its side, and the sound of everyone's gasps fills the room.

"Get the gun!" Jacob shouts to Ethan, but the only thing I can focus on is the woman lying there not moving. Her blue jeans are dirty and dusty, the flannel shirt on her torn in places. I push the bed against the wall as I take her in. I lean over, and I will never forget the sight of her face. If she wasn't beaten so badly, she would look like a sleeping doll.

One eye is swollen shut, and a cut on her cheek left a dried streak of blood. I pick up one of her hands, and her body feels like ice. My hand goes to her wrist to confirm she's alive. I feel the soft throb of her heartbeat ever so faint.

"There's another body in here. She's barely alive," I say into the radio. Looking over, I see they've already loaded Mayson's father onto the stretcher and draped a white sheet over him.

I slip one hand under her legs and another under her back, taking her in my arms.

Her head bobs like a rag doll as I turn to walk out of the cabin with her. As I approach the ambulance, I feel wetness hit my arm from her head. Looking down, I see her black hair is matted with blood.

"Oh my God." I hear my father say from beside me. "What the fuck?"

"She was under the bed," I say, my breath contracting in my chest as I step up in the ambulance and look at my father. "Get someone."

"The stretcher is inside," he says, and I see one of the EMTs running out.

"We need to transport the other guy," he says, huffing at me.

"The other guy is fucking dead!" I shout at him. "She has a chance, so either you get your ass in that chair and drive"—I motion with my head to the front—"or someone else will."

"I will," Ethan says from behind him. "You stay here and wait for the other bus."

"That isn't how this works," he says, and Ethan just looks past him as he closes one back door and then the other.

I hear the driver's door open and then close, and then the passenger door follows. "Hurry up!" I shout at them and then look down at the woman in my arms. "Don't give up," I say softly. "Don't you dare give up."

I don't even want to know what happened to her. The thought's too much to bear as I hold her in my arms, knowing she could take her last breath at any moment.

"Five minutes out!" Ethan shouts from the front.

"Did you hear that?" I say. "Five minutes and we are there."

She stirs in my arms. Her one eye slowly opens, and I see the greenest eyes I've ever seen. So crystal clear, it's like you can see right into her soul. "You're safe," I say as the ambulance stops, and she closes her eye.

Two

WILLOW

So much noise. I try to put my hands to my ears as I hear shouting, but my arms are so heavy I can't lift them. "Don't make a peep," I tell myself from under the bed. The coldness seeps into my bones like ice.

I look to the side, seeing the blonde we were following for the past couple of months slumped down on her side. Her eyes open once, and we make eye contact. Her mouth opens, and then her eyes shut the same time as mine do.

Footsteps stomp into the room, so close to me, and I try to open my eyes, but they are so heavy. I try to force them open or to scream, "I'm here. I'm here," but it's all for nothing. The more I open my mouth, the more nothing happens.

Someone is right next to me. I can feel their heat rush over me, and the coldness almost leaves me. My arm is being lifted and then more loud voices. My arm drops to my side, the heat of their hand gone.

I hear a soft voice, and I know I must be dreaming. There has never been a soft voice in my life in over eight years.

I open my eyes, and I'm in the middle of the forest. Turning around in a circle, I hear the soft voice again and I fight like hell to run toward it. I hear other voices around. Light shines through the leaves, and I hold out my hand to feel the heat from the sun. I smile and look up, feeling the sun on my face.

"Did you hear that?" His voice is so soft, yet feels so far away. "Five minutes and we are there." I hear the voice echo through the whole forest, and my body lights up. I run straight to the voice, and I'm surprised when my eyes open.

But instead of the darkness of the cabin, light is all around me. But I'm too busy staring into the bluest eyes I have ever seen. Blue like the ocean I've always dreamed about swimming in. Blue like the sky on a summer day with no clouds in the sky.

"You're safe." His voice is soft as he looks into my eyes. I take one look at him before the wave comes and sucks me under the water. My whole body feels like it's sinking, and when I open my eyes, I'm on a beach. Waves crash against the sand as I look up at the blue sky. The sun shines brighter than I've ever seen, and I close my eyes, basking in the heat.

A sense of peace settles over me as I lie here, feeling the warm water wash over my feet. My arms are stretched to the sides like a starfish, and my hands play in the sand. The little grains of the sand are scratchy when I rub my fingers together.

Opening my eyes, my gaze lands on the lone bird flying in the sky. "I'm not fucking leaving her!" Hearing someone shouting, I look right and left to see if anyone is on the beach with me, but all I see is sand and water.

"We don't have time for this!" someone else yells, and I feel the wetness of the water coming over my legs. I close my eyes and tilt my face up to the sky, feeling the sun's warmth.

"We're losing her," someone else says. I sit up, looking around at the emptiness of the beach, yet the voices are still coming. The crystal blue water matches the man's blue eyes.

The water goes as far as I can see it. "You need to let us work on her."

Where are those voices coming from? Looking around at nothing but sand and water, I get up, my feet sinking into the cold, wet sand. I take a deep inhale as the salty ocean rolls over my feet.

I run along the shore, just as I've dreamed of doing my whole life. It was my safe place I would escape to when I closed my eyes. I lean down and put my hands into the water and throw it up into the air, laughing as it falls back on my head.

This is my happiness. Being here and free is what I've always wished for. I kick the water up, and the sound of the waves crashing onto the shore get louder and louder. "I think we have a pulse."

I turn to look behind me, and I'm suddenly in the forest again. The sunlight fights to stream in among the green trees. I walk in the forest, the twigs snapping under my feet. I don't know how long I walk, but I'm just walking and walking, seeing the same trees.

Looking around, I try to find another way to go, yet no matter which way I turn, I land at this rock every single time.

I sit in the middle of the rock and cross my legs under me, looking at every single leaf there is. I look up at the sun that peeks through. "You're free." I smile and look down at my arms. The bruises from being tied to the bed are gone.

My finger rubs over the bruises I knew were there, and when I close my eyes this time, I'm back in the small shack where he kept me.

The devil. It's the only name that actually suits him. Eight years of hell. Eight years of living with the fear that tomorrow could be my last day. Eight years of wishing to die.

The leaves shake, the sound of swishing picks up, and I stand to walk over to the light coming in. It's so bright that I hold up my hand to block it from my eyes.

The gust of wind whips my hair in my face. I try to turn my head, but it sucks me into the light. "We're losing her," I hear a woman say frantically. "Her bp is falling."

"We need to get her into the OR!" another male's voice yells. Someone holds my hand up to my face, and the touch makes my whole hand tingle.

"You can't go with us," the woman says quietly.

"I'm going to be here when you wake up." I feel a soft touch on my cheek and open my eyes.

The bright light hits me right away, but the blue eyes hover over me. "I'll be right here," he says, and I close my eyes for just one more second. The heat from my face is gone, my hand turns back to ice, and when I open my eyes, I'm still in the forest. The sunlight is gone as the sound of beeping starts.

I sit down on the rock to make sure I'm ready for the strike that will come. The strikes always come at night.

I hold my legs to my chest, trying to warm myself, but I just shiver in the coldness. "Fight, baby girl." I hear my mother's voice, and I get up.

"Mom," I call her name, the tears running down my face.

"You need to fight with everything you have." Her voice comes stronger. "You are the strongest girl I know."

I look around the darkness as I try to walk to where the voice is coming from, but every time I step forward, I sink into the black earth. "She's flatlining."

"Mom!" I call her name again. "Come back for me!" I cry out. "Don't leave me again." The ache in my chest feels stronger than it has since she left me. "I can't do it without you."

"You can," she says, and I feel heat all over my body, almost as if she is giving me a hug. "You have to." The pressure on my chest gets stronger and stronger as my mother's voice gets farther and farther away from me. "You are so brave" is the last thing I hear from her before the beeping starts up again, this time getting louder and louder in my ears.

I hold my hands up to my ears to block it out. "That was close," someone says.

"We aren't out of the woods yet," the man's voice says, and I lie down in the darkness of the forest. My legs bend, and my arms are stretched out as the pain in my body comes back to me.

He's hit me before, but nothing like the last time. My arm snapped back so hard I knew my shoulder was dislocated as he hit me over and over again. The rage in him because I wouldn't do what he asked me to do. I wouldn't be a pawn in his game. The burning in my head returns, and I close my eyes just so I can fade to the blackness.

Three

QUINN

"It's been eight hours." I look over at the nurse who just stares at me. I've been coming to the desk every thirty minutes, and they've said the same thing over and over again. Two other nurses avoid my eyes as I stand here.

"And like I told you before," she says, looking at me. "As soon as we know something, we are going to let you know." She looks down at the chart in front of her.

Turning around, I run my hands through my hair and go back to the empty waiting room. It's been like this the whole night. Black chairs are set around the room with two vending machines. Two tables in the room hold newspapers that look like they've been thrown on them. The television is on, but there is no sound. I look out the window, seeing the sun has come up. The big window faces the parking lot with just a couple of cars parked there.

I watch the sun move up and replace the moon. The only thing in my head is the look of her eyes when she opened them and looked at me. I saw the look of horror. I saw the look of fear. I saw the look of a woman who was one step away from letting go.

"There he is." I turn and see my mother and father walk in with a tray of coffees. "We brought you coffee."

The second I got to the hospital, Mom was running to be with my aunt Savannah as my cousin Chelsea was being rushed into surgery. Slowly, the room filled up with everyone we could think to call, but then just as slowly, the room started to empty when the news came that Chelsea was out of surgery and waking up. Ethan had wanted to stay, but I forced him out of here when I looked over to see Emily holding their baby girl in her arms. The only ones who stayed with me were my parents.

We watched the seconds turn into minutes and then the minutes turn into hours. I finally kicked them out of here four hours ago. My mother didn't want to leave me, but my father dragged her out of here.

"Any news?" My mother sets the tray down and gives me a hug.

"Nothing," I say, shaking my head and grabbing the cup of hot coffee from the brown takeout container. I take a sip, ignoring the burning right down to my stomach.

Sitting down, I look down at my feet. I'm still wearing the black outfit from when I found her. The only thing I took off was the bulletproof vest.

"Honey," my mother says, and I look over at her. She wrings her hands together, and I know she is nervous about what she is going to say. "What are you doing here?"

"Darlin'," my father says. My parents met when my mother was running from her ex. She is from the city, and he is from the country. Watching them together is like watching oil and water mix.

"Don't you darlin' me, cowboy," she says, folding her arms over her chest. "I'm just asking the question everyone else is too afraid to ask." She turns and looks at me. "What the hell are you doing here?"

"Mom," I say, taking another sip of my coffee. "What do you expect me to do, just leave her here alone?" I ask. She opens her mouth to say something, but nothing comes out. "We don't even know who the fuck she is, let alone how to contact a family member to wait for her. Dying alone." I shake my head, trying to swallow down the lump in my throat. The same lump that has been there since she opened her eyes and looked at me. "No one deserves that, Mom."

She puts her hand on mine. "But you don't even know if she is a good person."

I look up at my father. "She has a point there. She was in the cabin." He runs his hands through his blond hair. They say I look exactly like him, but I'm a touch taller than he is.

"Under a fucking bed, beaten almost to death," I say, sitting up. "I doubt she would be in there fighting for her life if they were working together. What if she has parents out there looking for her?" I ask my mother. "What if a mother, just like you, is sitting down in her living room waiting for the phone to ring? What if it was Harlow?"

"I get the picture, Quinn," my mother says, wiping a tear away from her face.

"Did anyone contact the missing persons?" I look over at my father, knowing that if anyone can find out who she is, it would be him.

"I contacted a couple of friends of mine and put some feelers out there." He puts his hands on his hips. "But no one fitting her description has been reported as missing."

I shake my head. "I don't know what her story is, but something inside me tells me she has nothing to do with this."

"Or maybe you are too close to it to see what is right in front of you," my father says. Ever since I can remember, he has never been the one to sugarcoat things. He looks at things from both sides and sees the good and the bad in everyone. In his field, I guess he has to, and most times, we are butting heads about things. It's why I didn't follow in his footsteps. It's why instead of going into computers, I stuck to the farm life.

"Or maybe, just maybe she was held there and not given a choice," I counter, and my father just stares at me.

"Guys," my mother says, trying to calm us both down. "It's not the time or the place for this."

My father and I share a look, and I know that this conversation is far from over.

I'm about to say something else when I see the doctor coming out. His scrubs are full of blood as he looks down with a defeated expression.

"You need to rein it in," my father says, "I know that look, Quinn. You need to realize both of you are on the same side."

He talks to the nurse at the station, and she points over at us. "Oh my God," my mother says, slipping her hand into mine. Her nervousness is felt all the way to my bones. Her hand trembles in mine as she squeezes it tightly.

"Are you with Jane Doe?" the doctor asks us. I can't even say anything because my mouth is so dry. I watch him, wondering if he is going to tell us the worst-case news. Will he tell us that the woman I held in my arms died? Just the thought sends my heart into overdrive.

"She's alive." He cuts right to it. "Barely." My legs shake. "She coded three times." I release my mother's hand as I put my hand to my stomach. The pressure feels like an elephant is sitting on my chest.

"What is wrong with her?" my mother asks.

"What isn't wrong with her?" He shakes his head. "She had a massive head injury. I've never seen anything so bad. I stopped the bleeding there, but that is just the beginning. To be honest, I don't know how she's still alive." I open my mouth in shock. "The next forty-eight hours are going to be crucial for her. Even if she survives this, we still don't know the extent of her brain injuries."

"When can I see her?" I ask, and he looks down.

"It's supposed to be family only," he says, but he must see that no matter what he says, I'm not leaving here.

"Considering we are calling her Jane Doe and the fact no one else is here," my father says, "I'm going to go out on a limb and say we're the only family she has right now."

He nods his head. "Only one of you can go in."

"Thank you," I say, watching him turn around and walk away.

"Jesus," my mother says, walking to one of the chairs with shaky hands. "Quinn." She looks at me. "This is ..." She blinks away tears, putting her hand on the top of her head. Her own blue eyes are becoming a shade darker. "You can't do this." She looks at me and then at my father. "Cowboy," she says his nickname softly, and he just looks down.

"Mom," I say, and she holds up her trembling hand.

"You are going to sit by her bedside, and you don't even know her name. You don't even know her story," she says.

"I don't know what to say," I tell my mother honestly. "There is just something in me that can't just leave her here alone." Even if I tried to explain it, I don't think I would be able to. How do you explain that something inside me can't leave her? How do you explain that everything in your body yells at you to stay?

"She might die in there, and God knows how this will affect you." She uses the back of her hand to dab away her tears. "You always have this need to save things." She comes to me, putting her hand on my cheek. "Sometimes, you just need to watch instead of jumping all in."

"If you guys want to help." I look at her, then at my father. "Find out who she is."

"We're working on it," my father says. "But there was nothing in that cabin."

"What about the black bag?" I ask him about the bag I had in my hand when I first spotted her under the bed.

"Nothing in there but clothes and a locket," he says. "No wallet, no nothing."

"How can one person be so off the radar?" My mother looks at my father. "There has to be something in the system."

"Did we get her fingerprints?" I ask my father, and he shakes his head.

"There are so many prints in that cabin," he says, and I close my eyes. "It'll be a while before we get anything concrete."

"Well, then get me something, and I'll get them, and we can run them through the system." I point at where the blue doors are.

"What are you talking about?" My mother rises. "This woman is going to be fighting for her life. I will not let you go in there and do that."

"How else are we going to find out?" My father puts his hands on his hips.

"We'll find out when she wakes up and you ask her," my mother says. "You need to go home and shower." She looks at me, and I shake my head.

"I'm not leaving," I say.

"You have her blood on your hands," she says, and I look down at my hands. I hadn't even noticed.

"I'll wash up." I look at her.

"You can't go in there right now, and I promise I will stay here the whole time," she says, and she holds her hand up to my cheek. "My sweet boy. She's going to wake up alone and afraid and probably in a lot of pain. The last thing she'll want to see is you dressed all in black with her blood on you."

I look over at my father. "Give me your keys." I hold out

my hand, and he's about to hand me the keys when the nurse enters.

"Mr. Barnes," she calls my name and smiles at me. "You can come with me." She turns on her white hospital shoes and doesn't even look back to see if I'm following her.

I look over at my mother, who has tears in her eyes. "I don't want to leave you here," she says.

"I'll text you if I need you," I say and hug her. I slip my arms around her waist, and she looks up and kisses my cheek.

"You always were the one to help the wounded," she says, and then I look at my father.

"I'll let you know when she wakes up," I say, not thinking about the alternative.

I turn, following the nurse down the beige hallway right past the nurses' station that I went to earlier.

She presses the silver button on the wall, and the two blue doors open. Walking in, I feel it's a whole different space. All I hear is the beeping from the machines. Even the overhead light is dim on this side of the hospital.

A nurses' station sits in the middle of the huge room with a whiteboard behind them. Each room has a name except for one that has Jane on it. Her column is empty like a blank canvas.

Each room has a window that looks out to the nurses' station. She pushes open the door to the room, and I think I'm ready for what is to greet me.

But.

I. Was. Wrong.

I stop in the middle of the entrance as I look at her in the bed. The sound of the machine beeping beside her echoes in the room.

She lies in the middle of the bed, wearing a white and blue hospital gown. One hand rests at her side with a gray button on her finger, while the other arm is in a cast up to her elbow.

"She's stable," the nurse tells me, and I don't even turn my head away from the woman in the bed. Her face is as white as before but cleaned. One of her eyes is still swollen shut.

I take a step forward and stand next to her bed, a white bandage is around her head. A tube down her throat helps her breathe, and the only thing I can watch is her chest rising and falling. "Is she in pain?" I ask the nurse.

"No," she says, and I see the IV in her arm. "We are giving her morphine every four hours." I sit in the chair beside her bed. My eyes go to one of the machines with green lines on it. "I'll leave you alone. If you need me." I look over at her. "My name is Deborah."

I don't say anything to her because I don't trust my voice not to break. Instead, I nod at her, and she walks out of the room. I have never had to sit by someone's bed and watch them fight to live. I have never had the pull that I have to this woman who I know nothing about.

My hand moves to take hers in mine. Her icy hand sits in my big warm one. "I'm here," I say softly, and I hope she can hear me. "You're safe. I promise you."

Four

WILLOW

"The longer she sleeps, the better it is for her," I hear a woman say as I try to fight off the darkness. "It means her body is healing."

"She flinched her fingers yesterday," the man's voice says. "When is the doctor coming back?" His voice goes higher.

"He should be passing by soon," the woman says, and I sense that he's asked her this question before. "You can go home, and I can call you if it changes."

"I'm not going anywhere," he snaps, and then I hear footsteps walk away from the bed.

My arm is picked up. "I know you can hear me," he says, his tone softer than how he was with the nurse. "I saw your finger move. I know I did." I feel the heat over me, and I want to move my hand, but the darkness just comes and takes me away. His voice gets farther and farther away from me. "Open your eyes. Please."

I struggle to run from the blackness. I fight it with everything I have, and it's still too strong for me. My chest hurts from all the running.

"Her breathing is getting better." I hear the voice as I try to push the darkness away. "We are going to take out her breathing tube and see."

"Is that going to hurt her?" the soft voice asks as something rubs my hand.

"You are going to have to give me some space," the woman says, and the touch on my hand doesn't move.

"Oh, don't look at me like that," the man says. The woman laughs.

"You know, in the beginning, you sitting here the whole time was sweet. Now, you are just becoming a pain."

He's been sitting here the whole time? Why? I wonder. Why is he still here?

"Before I start this," the woman says, "I need you to know that she might be in just a touch of pain." I feel tugging on my chest.

"Why is her heart speeding up?" The man's voice is frantic.

"It's coming back down," she says, huffing out. "If you guys ever have children"—she laughs—"I want to sit in the waiting room and watch."

The pain in my throat goes away and then I feel little touches on my hand.

I hear the beeping, and the sound comes closer and closer as I move toward the rock. My eyes fly open, but one is still sealed shut. I look around frantically, not sure where I am. My breaths come out almost in pants as I fight off the heaviness of my eyes. The pain hits me right away and knocks the air right out of me.

I try to get my heart rate down just a bit as I look around the room. Hospital room. The light from outside hits me right away, and I close my eye again. The pain in my head is making me keep it closed just a touch longer as it shoots to my stomach.

I open my eye slowly as I take in the room. My eyes go from the closed door to the corner of the room that faces the window. The blinds are also closed but the sunlight fights to come in.

I close my eyes, trying to pick up my hand, but it's too heavy. I swallow, and the burning makes me close my eyes to catch my breath.

When my eyes open again, they're not as heavy as the last time, but my head continues to pound. I look around the room and stop when I see him sitting in the chair. He has his head back, and his eyes are closed. His hands are folded over his chest while his long legs are stretched out in front of him. His hair is lighter than it was in the dark. His black clothes are gone and in their place are blue jeans with a gray T-shirt. My heart speeds up this time, scared that this man is still here. Why is he still here? My fingers start to move up and down with the nerves inside me. I look around, wondering how I could escape. I try to lift my leg just a touch, but nothing moves.

Was his voice the one I've been hearing?

I lick my dry lips as I fight to keep my eyes open. The heaviness is coming on strong. I close my eyes just to rest them for a second, slowly blinking, but they remain shut.

I don't have the energy to open them again, but this time, the darkness comes with a vengeance.

The beeping from the machines lulls me back to sleep.

"Did you eat?" I hear a woman's voice, and my eyes flicker open.

I want to open my eyes longer, but my body just sinks into the bed, and I drift off.

"It's been four days," he says angrily. "You said twenty-four to forty-eight hours." Four days, I repeat to myself. Have I really been asleep for four days? That is impossible. I must have heard wrong.

"I said that those hours were critical," another man says. "The swelling in her brain has gone down. That is amazing news. That she is still alive is a miracle. I'll see you tomorrow."

I moan, hoping that they hear me. I try to lift my hands, but it feels like I have concrete in them. *I'm here*, I yell. My voice is screaming in my head.

The sound of his shoes are moving away from me. "I'm going to need you to open your eyes, please." His voice is close to me. My hand is getting hot from being in his. "Show me those green eyes."

I force my eyes to open to show him my eyes. I force my eyes to open so I can make sure he's not waiting for me in a dark corner to pull me out of this bed and drag me back to the place he calls home. Which is my hell, where I spent the past eight years trying to escape. Every single time being sucked back in.

"I just need to know you're okay," he says, and I feel a prickle on my hands. "Anything?" he asks, and I force myself to squeeze his hand.

"You can't run from me." I hear the evil voice as I run through the forest, branches hitting me in the face. My legs get heavier and heavier as I run. I look over my shoulder as he chases me. The branches sting as they scrape my legs.

His hands try to grab me, but I run out of his grasp. "When I get you," he hisses, "I'm going to make sure I finish the job."

I gasp, opening my eyes, looking around the room frantically to see where I am. My eyes land on the man who carried me out of the cabin. My chest heaves as I catch my breath. "Oh my God," he says, his hand squeezing mine a little as I try to calm my heartbeat.

"You're safe," he says, his blue eyes darker than I saw them last time. The circles under his eyes look like he hasn't slept in days. "You're safe," he repeats. My heart still races, and I look around the room, checking to see who else is here with me.

I lick my lips, wanting to say something, but my throat is

scratchy. "Don't talk," he says, getting up and rushing over to the door. I look around, wondering if I can go out by the window. I take in the whole room and make an escape plan. I try to move my legs, and this time, it moves up but immediately crashes back on the bed.

I close my eyes as my head starts to pound again, then force my eyes open again. "She's up, I swear," he says loudly. He comes back into the room with a smile on his face. "See?" He points at me. "I told you."

"Hi," the nurse says with a big smile, and I look at her. So many questions come to mind. But the main one has nothing to do with her or me.

"Head." I start to croak out, licking my lips and then closing my eyes. I lift my hand that doesn't have a cast on it to my head, touching the white bandage. The pounding makes me close my eyes to try to push it away. "Hurts." I try to wet my tongue.

"That's good," the nurse says. She walks over to a table and brings me a Styrofoam white cup with a straw in it. "Take little sips," she says, and I take a sip.

The burning down my throat makes me stop for one second. My eyes are on the man who stands at the foot of my bed, watching me like a hawk. I try to sit up, but the pain pushes me back like someone just kicked me in the stomach. "You are going to hurt yourself," the man says, and I hold up my hand as it shakes like a leaf on a tree in a windstorm.

I put my hand down and take another sip of water. The cool water makes my tongue feel less heavy. I look at the nurse, who just looks at me as I try to tell her with my eyes. "Do you know where you are?" she asks me, and I look at the man in front of me.

He is the most handsome man I've ever seen. He almost looks like one of those princes in fairy tales. "Who are you?"

Five

QUINN

"Who are you?" she asks in a voice that sounds like she has laryngitis. I look at her green eyes, and no matter how many times I pictured her eyes in my head, nothing compares to the sight when she opens them.

"I'm going to get the doctor," Shirley, the nurse, says. She turns and stops beside me. "You might want to be nice to her." I roll my eyes. "Nicer than you are to everyone else." I put my hands on my hips, but my eyes never leave hers.

For the past four days, I've sat in that fucking chair, making sure her chest moved. I would doze off and hear her calling my name and wake scared to death that she died while I was sleeping.

"Who are you?" she asks me again as she taps her finger nervously on the bed beside her.

"Who are you?" I ask her the question that I've waited over four days to ask her. The endless questions are killing me every single day I don't have an answer.

I'm about to ask her again when Shirley comes back into the room. "Okay," she says a bit too loudly, and the girl in the bed jumps with fear. Shirley's eyes go to her and then to me.

"It's okay. It's just me." She holds up her hands. "I've paged the doctor."

The girl in the bed just looks at her, trying to get her breathing under control. "I'm going to take your vitals." Shirley walks over to her, putting the blood pressure machine on her small, frail arm. She puts her stethoscope in her ears. The girl in the bed looks down to see what she's doing. When she sees, she looks back up at me for just a second before her eyes roam around the room again to every single corner.

"It's a little high," Shirley says as she unclips the Velcro strap from her arm. "But that is normal."

The woman just nods at her, and I stand here trying to take her in. Fuck, maybe I have been looking at this in the wrong way. Maybe she's so jumpy because she's guilty.

The door opens again, and this time, it's the doctor. But the woman just sees a man, and she turns to get out of the bed. My feet work faster than my head, and I catch her right before she hits the floor.

The arm with the cast grips my arm, her nails digging into my skin. "I got you," I whisper, my face so close to hers I can feel her breathing all over me. My heart speeds up a touch with her hands on me, and I want to smile at her and tell her that everything is going to be okay. I want to tell her that I'm not going to let anyone hurt her. I want to hold her in my arms and make her feel safe.

"Oh my God!" Shirley shrieks, making the girl jump even more.

"I have to get out of here." She looks around as I pick her up and put her back into the bed.

She winces out in pain as she looks down at my arms as I place her back in the bed. "She's in pain," I tell the doctor, who just looks on in shock at what happened.

"I'm fine," she hisses, moving away from me and my touch as if I was poison.

"Well then," Dr. Benson says, coming closer to her. Her eyes open, and she tries to get out of the bed again.

I put my hand up to stop him from moving forward. "Back up a second. She's scared shitless," I say. My voice comes out louder than I want it to be, and she tries to move away from me again. "I'm not going to hurt you," I say between clenched teeth.

Shirley slaps her hands together, getting everyone to look at her. "Okay, one." She looks at me. "Move away from her and go stand over there." She points at the chair I've been sitting in for the past four days.

I slept maybe a total of an hour. My whole body was tense as we waited for this stranger to open her eyes and give us some answers. The nurses tried to get me to leave, tried to get me to just step outside and feel the air, but I stuck to my guns about not moving. There was no way I was going to leave her alone. Imagine if she woke up without anyone here. From the look that she gave me before, she would have hightailed it out of here. "Fine," I say, lifting my hands up so she can see them as I step back from her.

"I'd ask him to leave," Shirley says to the woman, "but he won't listen to that one." Shirley tries to get a smile out of the woman, but nothing comes out. She just looks at her like a bird looking to get away from its captor. "Now this man here ..." She looks at the woman. "His name is Dr. Benson, and he's been taking care of you since you got here." Her eyes go from Shirley to Dr. Benson, who stands there in his white lab coat with his hands in his pockets. His chest pocket is full of pens, and his stethoscope hangs around his neck.

"I'm Dr. Benson," he says. "Do you know where you are?"

"Hospital," she says, her eyes closing and then slowly opening.

"Your body needs to recuperate," he says. "But that you are even talking is ..."

"Can you cut to the chase and tell her what is wrong with her?" I snap. "Can't you see she's tired?"

"Then I suggest she rest," Dr. Benson says. "I'm going to guess that you will be awake again soon."

"I," she says, licking her lips. "He's …" She fights with everything she has. "Coming."

I walk to the bed as her eyes open wide when she sees me, but then shuts again. "He's not coming," I say softly. "He can't hurt you." Her eyes don't open again, and I look at the machine, seeing that her heart is beating normally.

"What the fuck was that?" I look over at Dr. Benson and Shirley.

"That," Shirley says, "was a woman who woke up confused and traumatized." She shakes her head. "You need to step out of here and let her get comfortable."

"Not a chance in hell," I say. "I was the one who held her in my arms while she fought to live. As long as she is here, this is where I'm staying."

I swallow and look down, the heat rising to my neck as I say the next words. "Did you guys check to see if …?" My body is one big bundle of nerves, and I'm not moving.

"She was not," Shirley says. "We checked."

"This woman," Dr. Benson says. "She was beaten so severely her brain started to bleed," he says softly. "She had three fractured ribs, and it wasn't the first time they were fractured. So the abuse was ongoing. Not to mention, her spleen had to be removed. Her wrist was snapped, and that doesn't happen from a fall. Someone purposely snapped it." He shakes his head. "That she can even talk is a miracle. You know that, right?" He looks straight at me. "I don't know how this all happened, and I can only imagine her story, but what I do know is that you coming in here freaking out is not helping anyone, least of all her."

I swallow down the lump in my chest. "I would never ever hurt her."

"Then I suggest you show her that you aren't going to blow up every ten seconds," Shirley says. "Hopefully, she wakes up again soon." She turns and walks out of the room with Dr. Benson following her.

I sit in the chair and look at her. I take my phone out this time and dial my father.

"Hey," he answers right away.

"Hi," I say softly, getting up and walking away from her. Going to the door, I step outside into the hallway. I stand in front of the window that looks inside her room. "She woke up."

"And?" he asks, and I close my eyes.

"Nothing. She was so fucking scared she tried to get off the bed," I say, looking at the woman sleeping. The woman who was awake for ten minutes maybe fifteen, yet I couldn't get her fucking name.

"Jesus," my father hisses, and I close my eyes and hang my head low. "Did she say anything?"

I huff out. "The only thing she asked is who I was."

"Did she tell you who she was?" my father asks anxiously.

"No," I answer, defeated. "Dad," I say, almost pleading. "Please tell me you have something."

"Son," he says, his voice going low, "I wish I could."

"What the fuck is going on?" I hiss, my patience gone. "How the fuck do you have all those people there, yet no one can find out who this woman is?"

"I am not your enemy," he says. "We are on the same team." I pinch the bridge of my nose.

"How is it that with all of our people, we can't find out who this woman is?" I ask.

"That is the question that we are asking ourselves," he huffs

29

out. "I've been in this office for the last four days," he says, "following a paper trail that keeps leading us to a dead end. You pick up one rock, and another ten get thrown at me." I shake my head. "We have guys going to interview everyone that has lived next to them, and everyone is saying only two people lived there."

"Someone has to know who this woman is," I say. "She's been with him for long enough that someone would have seen her."

"How do you know she was with him a long time?" my father asks, and my stomach burns when I think about what Dr. Benson said.

"She had fractured ribs," I say, and he knows I'm not done. "It wasn't the first time."

He hisses. "Motherfucker."

"Good news," I say. "It doesn't look like she was …" I look around the room. The nurses' station is empty, and the whiteboard in back has been written on. I listen to the sound of the machines coming from the other rooms. "Bring me a computer."

"For?" he asks me.

"I'll see if I can find something. I'm here doing nothing, so I might as well keep busy," I say.

"I didn't even think you knew what a computer did," he says.

"Just because I don't sit at the desk doesn't mean I don't watch," I say, smiling. "I'm my father's son in more ways than one."

"I tell you what you don't get from your father," he says, and I can just picture him with a smile on his face.

"Yeah, and what's that?" I put my head back, waiting for him to say something.

"Your patience," he says. "Or the lack of patience." I hear him tap on the desk. "You get that from your mother." I laugh. "But seriously, Quinn"—his voice goes low—"you need to know everyone has the same goal in mind, and that is to find out who this woman is." He doesn't say anything more to me. "I'll drop off a computer on my way home."

"Thanks, Dad," I say and hang up the phone. I walk back into the room as the sun from outside starts to set.

Walking over to the chair, I sit down next to her bed. I watch her chest rise and fall.

Her face is so pale, her cheekbones sticking out just a touch. I take her hand in mine and notice that it's warmer than it was before. I sit here waiting for her to open her eyes. I have so many more questions than I had before. Questions only she has the answers to. But the biggest one has to be her identity. "Who are you?" I ask her quietly.

Six

WILLOW

"Who are you?" I hear him ask me again, but this time, I can't open my eyes.

I feel his hand on mine, and I look around the darkness to see if I can see his eyes again. The way he watched me without saying anything. The nervous way he ran to catch me. His warm arms made heat run right through my body. I had this sudden feeling he would make sure I was safe. I clung to him, my nails digging into his arm, and he didn't even bat an eye. He just gently put me back on the bed as his eyes looked right into my soul.

The nurse made him go stand away from me, and I saw that he wanted to argue with her, but he went and stood aside. His eyes never leaving me.

The pain in my head comes on so strong that I moan. I slowly open my eyes once and try to look around, but my eyes fall closed again. I put my head back on the pillow, and the pain hits again. I flick my eyes open again and look straight at the yellow wall. The room is a lot darker than it was the last time. I turn to look out the window, but the shades are closed with no sun trying to peek in. "Hey," I hear the man say and close my eyes again as I try to get the heaviness out of them. I move my hand into a fist to try to keep myself up.

My head feels like someone is pounding on it with a jackhammer. I take a deep breath, but my side hurts so much. Breathing hurts, so I start to hold my breath and then pant out.

Maybe trying to get away from everyone and almost falling out of the bed was not my best idea. "I'm going to get Doris," he says, and I open my eyes. He's putting down a computer on the window ledge with the screen turned away from me. "She's the night nurse." He smiles at me. "She likes me better than Shirley." His blue eyes go just a touch lighter when he smiles, just like when the sun hits the blue water, making it almost crystal clear.

Why is he still here? I ask myself as I close my eyes again.

He turns to walk out of the room, but all he does is open the door and then whisper-shouts Doris's name. With his back turned to me, I take a minute to wince from the pain. Closing my eyes, I try to count to ten and then open them back up. My whole body aches from the top of my head to the tip of my toes.

I have never felt so much pain in my whole life. And God knows I've had my fair share of backhands and punches.

When he turns back around, I put on my poker face. I've never been in this much pain before, so I don't even know what type of poker face I have at the moment. "Do you want some water?" he asks, his voice softer than I've ever heard.

"No," I say, not willing to show anyone that I need anything. The minute you show them that you need or want things, they use that as a bargaining tool. I learned that eight years ago. I also learned that you can't trust anyone, not even your own mother.

"Your lips are dry," he says. "The water will help."

I want to tell him to leave, but the sharp pain in my head

33

makes me close my eyes as I try to control it. His face looks like it feels my pain, and he's about to say something when the nurse comes in. She looks friendlier than the last one, but the last one made sure no one came close to me. Even him.

She is wearing blue scrub pants, but her scrub top is white with cats all over it. "I was wondering if you would wake up for me." She smiles and comes over to me. "How are we doing?" Her black hair is pulled back in a ponytail. She has white hair around her temples, her stethoscope hangs around her neck, and her glasses sit on the edge of her nose.

"Fine," I say, trying to steady my heartbeat because the machine is picking it up. His eyes go from me to the machine and then back to me.

Her brown eyes look up at me from her glasses. "Is that so?" She tilts her head to the side. "So you don't feel like you've been hit by a truck?"

I want to laugh because not only does it feel like I got hit by a truck but it feels like a bus and a whole motorcade were after it. "I'll be fine."

"Do you want me to up your pain medicine?" she asks, walking over to the hanging IV bag and doing something to it.

"No," I tell her. "It makes me groggy."

"It allows your body to heal," she says.

"She said she doesn't want it," he says, his voice nothing like when he talks to me.

She looks over at him, and I'm expecting her to tell him to take a seat, but she shakes her head. "I'm going to go and see if I can get you some Jell-O."

She turns to walk out of the room, leaving me alone with the stranger. I try to sit up, but the sharp pain from my left side makes me stop moving.

I look over at him, and his eyes have never left mine. He steps forward as he stands beside the bed. "If you are feeling pain, you should tell her." His voice softens as he sits in the chair beside my bed and puts his hand on mine. The heat of his hand warms me up. "Your body has been through a lot."

"I said I'm fine," I almost hiss out. "Now, before I get sucked under again." I lick my lips, and I wish I did have water. The dryness of my mouth makes my tongue feel thick. "How long have I been here?"

He doesn't answer me. Instead, he walks out of the room, and I watch him. I look down at the hand in a cast and then fist the other one. I try to sit up, but the left side pulls again, making me wince.

"Here," he says, coming back in with a white Styrofoam cup. "It's ice water. The coolness will help your throat." I look at him and then the straw and then back at him. "Four days," he says. "I've been by your bedside almost five days. If I wanted to hurt you ..." He leans in, bringing the straw closer to my lips. "I would have."

His words roll around in my head. His hand never moves from in front of my mouth. I open my mouth, placing the straw between my lips, and take a little sip. He was right. The cool water makes my mouth and throat feel amazing. "Thank you."

He nods at me. "Okay, shall we, then?" I look at him. "Let's play twenty-one questions. What's your name?"

"What's yours?" I ask back, ignoring the throbbing from my wrist.

"Quinn," he says softly. "Now it's your turn." I look at this man who doesn't even know my name, yet he sat by my bed for the past four days.

"My name is Willow," I say softly and then look down. "Where am I?"

"Hospital twenty minutes out of Clarkstown," he says, and I start to think of where that is. The past five months have been a roller-coaster ride, if I'm honest. We didn't stay in the same spot for more than three days. I spent more than nine straight days sleeping in the car, and then we spent a month in that fucking cabin.

"The blond woman," I say, looking at him. "Is she okay?"

"Her name is Chelsea," he says. "She's going to be fine. He shot her in the shoulder." My eyes go big. "Went right through. Her wrist is also broken."

I put my head back and close my eyes as the relief that she is okay washes through me. "I tried to warn everyone," I say. "I tried to run, but he caught me and ..." I stop talking when I look down to see my hands shaking. I don't even know, but my hand goes to the side of my leg. I'm even afraid to look under and see the damage he left. He always made sure to put the bruises where no one could see. He was good at that.

I watch his eyes as I ask the next question. "How is ...?" I don't even want to say his name, and my heart speeds as the monitor picks it up. I look around, afraid he might be in this hospital right now. Afraid he'll pop up when I least expect it. Just like he always did.

Quinn sees it, too. "He's dead."

I open my mouth to say something, but nothing comes out. "Wh—" I start to say. My mouth gets drier and drier as I try to comprehend what he just said to me.

"He's dead," he repeats. "Lifted a gun and tried to shoot Mayson, and the sheriff shot him."

"You were there?" My heart goes around and around at the thought that I'm finally fucking free. He's dead, and he can't hurt me. Nothing is holding me back. I'm free.

The tears sting my eyes, and no matter how much I fight it, a lone tear falls over my bottom eyelid. I lift my hand and wince in the action. I close my eyes, and another tear comes out. "I'm sorry for your loss," he says, and I open my eyes to look at him.

"My loss?" I ask, not sure I heard him right. "Are you the police?" I ask him. "Is that why you are here stuck to my bed?

Do you need a statement from me?" I snap at him. "Or am I under arrest?" My hands get clammy, and my heart rate goes up even more. The back of my neck gets hot, and my stomach feels a burning sensation in it.

"How much pain are you in?" I open my eyes and look at him as he stands there with his arms across his chest. His arms look bigger.

"I'm fine," I say.

"Bullshit," he says, his voice going just a touch louder than before.

He's about to say something else when Doris comes back in with a bowl in her hands. "I found one." She holds up her arm.

"She's in a lot of pain," Quinn says, and I look at Doris.

"It's not that bad," I say, and I look over at Quinn.

"Stop being so stubborn and tell her how you really feel." He shakes his head.

"On a scale of one to ten," Doris says, "how much pain do you feel?"

"Zero," I lie to her. Quinn huffs, but instead of saying anything, he just walks out of the room.

"Okay, he's gone now," Doris says. "Tell me the truth."

"I'm fine," I say, and she looks at me.

"No one is going to think less of you for feeling pain."

I turn my head and watch Quinn from the window as he stands there with the phone to his ear. No doubt calling whoever he needs to call to give them a rundown of our conversation. Just another person in my life who needs something from me.

"Are the police outside my door?" I ask her, and she looks at me confused. Her eyebrows furrow.

"The police?" she repeats the question.

I close my eyes as the pain gets to be too much, and my

face grimaces. "I need to get out of here," I say, and she looks at me.

"I'm sure eventually you will." She smiles, and I just look at her.

Sooner than you think, I say to myself as I sit back and make my escape plan.

Seven

QUINN

I walk out of the room before I snap at her. Reining it in, I watch her through the window. My whole body shakes with anger as I watch Doris with her.

She looks at Doris and then looks at me, her eyes flying away from mine when she sees me looking at her. I take the phone out of my pocket and call the only person I know who can help me right now.

"Hey," my father says after half of a ring.

"Hey," I say back. "Her name is Willow." Her name falls off my lips like I've been saying it my whole life.

"Is she awake?" he asks, and I hear him moving around.

"She is." I look back at her and see her close her eyes and put her head back on the pillow.

"Did she give you a last name?" he asks.

"No, and I didn't ask her, to be honest." I look around to see if anyone else is in the hallway.

"What else did she say?" he asks.

"Not much. She asked if Chelsea was okay." I swallow. "She said she tried to warn her. But ..." I swallow down the rage coming right through me. "But he caught her before she could warn us."

"Fuck," he hisses and says the same thing I was thinking when I heard it. Actually, when I heard her say that, I thought it was a good thing he was dead because I would find him and finish the job.

"She also didn't know he was dead," I say.

"Do you think they were working together?" he asks, and just the thought makes my skin crawl. "Step out of the bubble for a minute," he says. "Do you think she was working with him?"

"No," I answer him honestly, and then I close my eyes and pray I'm not wrong. "Not with the way she is acting. She is too jumpy to be in on it. Besides, her injuries tell us a different story."

"But did you ask her?" he asks, and I wish I had another answer for him.

"I didn't have a chance to." I stop talking as I look at her smile for the first time. Not a whole smile, but a small side smile. Her green eyes light up just a touch. Unlike when she gets into her head, and she's alone with her thoughts. Then they get so clouded over.

"What is it?" my father asks, his voice low and calm but also full of worry.

"She's in fucking pain," I say through clenched teeth, my voice as low as it can go. "Fucking pain and she refuses to admit it."

"Quinn," he says my name, and I'm not sure if it's a warning or not. "Why don't I send someone to take your place for a couple of hours? You can go and get some sleep."

I ignore what he just said. "Dad, she is in so much pain her body shakes, and she doesn't even notice it." My stomach turns over as I look back into the room and see her eyes are still closed. "She is in so much pain that she holds her breath as she fights through it. She is in a fuck ton of pain, and she is jumpy and scared shitless." I don't tell him that she looks around every five seconds to make sure she knows where the exits are. I don't tell him that I have a feeling if she is left alone, she will try to run. I don't know her, but I feel it in my bones that she isn't going to stick around.

"Maybe it's you," he says, and I look down at the floor as I listen to him. "Maybe it's the fact you're a man, and she isn't comfortable with men. I could send in Amelia," he says. "See if she talks to her."

"No," I say. "Right now, she knows I'm here and not leaving. Sooner or later, she'll trust me."

"But what if she doesn't?" I close my eyes, not willing to think about that. "We don't know anything about her."

"We know she tried to get to Chelsea to help her, and we know that he left her for fucking dead." My voice goes lower. "If she was in on it, why would he leave her for dead?" I ask him the same question my head has been asking me. "Why hide her under a fucking bed?"

"I have no idea," my father huffs. "There are so many questions still unanswered."

"Well"—I look over at the woman in the bed—"all the answers are there." I look down and then up again, not adding that she just has to give them to us.

"I'm going to ask her more when she is up to it," I say. "In the meantime, see if anyone has mentioned her name anywhere."

"I'll send it to Derek." My father mentions his second-in-command. "If anyone can find out who she is, he can."

"I'll check on my end also," I say. "I'll let you know."

"Quinn," he says. "What is going on here?" he asks me. "You find this girl, and then you stick by her like glue."

"She has no one," I remind him.

41

"This isn't one of the horses you rescue," he says. "Not all of them can be saved."

"This isn't that," I say, and he laughs.

"Son, you are talking to someone who has known you your whole life," he says. "You are the most nurturing soul I know. You see the wounded, and all you want to do is make it better."

"This isn't like that," I say, but even I don't believe the words coming out of my mouth.

"I'll let you know what I find out on my end," he says, not willing to have this conversation with me right now. "Let me know how things go on your end."

"I will," I say, hanging up and looking over to see Mayson standing there talking to the nurse.

Looking into the room, I see her eyes are still closed, and Doris comes out of the room. "How is she doing?"

"She's a fighter," she says, looking back into the room and seeing her eyes are closed. "I just upped her pain meds."

"Did she ask for it?" I ask Doris, and she just looks at me.

"She said she was fine," she says. "But then you saw her erratic heartbeat every time she felt pain."

"How long is she going to be out?" I ask Doris.

"She should be out for about four hours," she says and walks away from me, going over to the whiteboard and writing numbers on it.

"Her name is Willow," I tell Doris, and she looks over her shoulder at me. "You can change the Jane Doe." I point at the top of her column. With a smile, she erases Jane Doe and replaces it with Willow.

"She has a name?" Mayson says from beside me.

"She does," I say. "How is Chelsea?"

"She thinks she is leaving tomorrow." He shakes his head.

"Do you know her?" I ask him. To be honest, things between Mayson and me have not always been smooth. I didn't trust him when he first got here, and I still don't trust him. But, and there is a huge but, Chelsea has chosen him. So I have to respect her and accept him, if for no one else but her.

"Never seen her in my life," he says, looking into the room again.

"When you were held captive"—I look at him to see if his eyes flicker—"do you think she was there?"

He looks at me, his eyes hard as he folds his arms across his chest. "I was tied to a tree," he says, his voice tight.

"Did you see her maybe in the cabin?" I ask.

"I didn't see anyone but my father," he says, "but that isn't to say she wasn't there."

"She said she tried to run away and warn Chelsea," I start to tell him, "and then he caught her."

He shakes his head. "Nothing you say will surprise me."

"There you are." I look to the right and see Chelsea walking toward us very slowly.

"What are you doing out of bed?" Mayson asks, looking around to see if there is a wheelchair he can grab.

"I'm tired of lying around doing nothing," she huffs out. "I'm fine. I can lie in bed at home." She looks at me. "You look like shit."

"Right back at you," I say, and she laughs. She comes over to me, and I hug her.

"Watch her shoulder," Mayson tells me, and I just look at him. Chelsea, Amelia, and I grew up together, almost like triplets. In school, it was always the three of us. They are my best friends; they know me better than I know myself.

"Did she wake up?" Chelsea asks, looking into the room where Willow sleeps.

"For a bit," I tell her. "Her name is Willow," I say, and she looks over at the chart on the wall.

"Her heartbeat is all over the place. She must be in pain,"

Chelsea says, her medical training kicking in. "They upped her pain meds but not by much."

"She says she's fine," I say, and she looks at me with her mouth open.

"They drilled a hole in her head to reduce the swelling. I can confirm with you from other patients that I've had that she is in a fuck ton of pain. That isn't even counting all her other injuries."

"Did you see her?" Mayson asks Chelsea. "At the cabin."

"No." She shakes her head. "I told you, I told Uncle Casey, and I've told Uncle Jacob over and over again. He was alone. Drove the car alone. Carried me alone. In the cabin, he was alone. I had no idea she was even there."

"We should get you into bed," Mayson says, and she tries to pretend she isn't tired, but the yawn that escapes her tells us otherwise.

"Go rest. I'll come and get you tomorrow when she gets up, and we can hear her story," I say. "Maybe she can answer our questions."

"Well, the other person is sitting on ice in the morgue," Mayson says.

"It's a good thing," I say. "Because if he wasn't, I don't know what I would do."

Chelsea looks over at me, and her eyebrows pinch together. I know she wants to ask me questions, but she doesn't. I also know she is saving it for another day when she can sit down with me and see if I'm lying to her. It was something we did when we were kids, and as we grew, we were able to see when someone was lying to us. "I'll see you tomorrow," she says, and Mayson holds her hand as they walk back to her room.

I walk back into the room, stopping at the foot of her bed to look at her. The monitor shows her heart is beating steadily.

She lies there so peaceful with her chest moving up and down rhythmically.

Making my way over to the chair beside her bed, I reach out and grab her hand. It's small and fragile and cold. I put my other hand on it to warm her up. One hand holds her while I use the other one to rub her finger. My index finger rubbing hers, I'm tempted to bring her hand to my lips and softly kiss it. "Willow," I say her name softly. "What secrets are you keeping?" I ask.

Eight

WILLOW

My eyes flicker open, and I take a deep breath. The pain in my head is just a bit less than it was last night. I woke up three times during the night, and each time I woke up, he was by my side.

His eyes on his computer, he would get up and make sure I was okay. I wanted to tell him to leave. I wanted to get the nurse to get him to leave, but the darkness came to take me away before I could do any of those things.

I fight the sleep off and look at the chair, and for the first time, he isn't there. My heart speeds up, and I can't stop it. My breathing comes faster and faster as if I'm running a marathon. My mind runs in overdrive as I take in the empty room and suddenly feel all alone. I've been wishing for him to be gone, and when he is, I don't feel as safe. I push the thought away. *The only one you can count on, Willow, is yourself,* I remind myself over and over again.

Glancing around the room, I look for where I can escape, and then I see him. Standing in the hallway with a blonde who smiles up at him. She gets on her tippy toes and kisses his cheek and then turns to walk away from him. He stands there

46

watching her walk away from him. I swallow down the sudden lump in my throat as I watch him walk back into the room.

"Good morning," he says, and I see the big brown bag in his hand.

"What time is it?" I ask.

"Just after nine," he says, putting the bag down on the hospital tray. "How are you feeling?"

"Groggy," I answer him honestly. "But I'm fine." He just looks at me with his hands on his hips, and I see he's wearing a different shirt. Maybe he did leave when I was sleeping.

"I'll get Shirley," he says between his teeth, almost hissing.

"Good morning, Willow," Shirley says, coming in, and I wait for Quinn to follow her, but he doesn't. He just stands outside the room, looking in.

"Good morning," I say, and she comes to me and takes my vitals.

"How are you this morning?" she asks.

"Fine," I say, and she looks at me over her glasses.

"Um, Shirley," I say her name softly as I look out to see Quinn still standing there watching. I move my head back to make sure he won't see me. "Why is he here?"

"He hasn't left here since you got here," she says. "He takes off for twenty minutes each night to take a shower."

My mouth opens. "What day is it?"

"Friday," she says, and she looks at me. "Now answer me honestly, and I promise not to tell anyone." I swallow, not sure I can actually answer the truth to anyone. "How are you really feeling?"

I look down. "I'm in a little bit of pain," I admit and don't meet her eyes. Just in case she sees that a little bit means a lot.

"Where does it hurt?" she asks, her voice so soft it's like we're whispering to each other. She puts her hand on my arm to make me feel safe.

"My head throbs," I say. "Side feels like someone is stabbing me, and then on the other side, it feels like I'm being kicked." Tears sting my eyes, and I lift my hand and hiss out at the pain shooting all the way up to my shoulder.

"Did your arm hurt when you lifted it?" she asks, and I want to tell her yes, but I look down at my lap.

"It's not that bad." I ignore the thumping of my heart as I try to block out the pain.

"I'll be back," she says, and I grab her arm, surprising her.

"Don't tell anyone," I beg, fearing she will tell someone how much pain I'm in. "I'm fine."

"Willow," she says, her voice very low. "No one is going to know what you told me," she says. "But I think you need an X-ray just to make sure everything is okay."

"But ..." I look from her to Quinn, who sees my face and comes charging in.

"What's the matter?" he asks, his tone going from low to loud.

"Nothing is the matter," Shirley says before I do. "She's fine. But the doctor ordered some tests, so I was telling her about them."

"What kind of tests?" he asks, his face full of worry. "He hasn't been here this morning."

My mouth is suddenly dry as I hear the galloping of my heart in my ears. "It is a routine test," Shirley says. "Stop asking me questions; I'm taking care of her," she huffs and walks past him. "Don't make me hurt you," she says to him, and he rolls his eyes as she walks out.

"Why do I feel like she's lying to me?" He looks at me, his eyes never wavering from mine.

"I don't know anything about you," I say. "So I have no idea why you would think that. But if I did, I would just say that you're paranoid and have too much time on your hands." I shrug my shoulders, and I almost cry out in pain.

My lower lip trembles, and he sees the pain this time. I

expect him to say something to me, but he doesn't have the chance because Shirley comes back in. "Okay, let's get you going," she says, coming to me and unclipping things and then unlocking the wheels. "Let's take you for a ride," she says with a smile. "We'll be back in about thirty minutes."

He just nods at her as she wheels me out of the room. "Thank you," I say softly when we are far enough from the room for him to hear.

"You don't have to thank me for doing my job," she says and pushes me through the blue doors. The lights shine in from the windows as we roll down the beige hallway.

My eyes go crazy as I look around at the people coming and going. My palms get sweaty from my nerves, and I fear that he could pop up at any time. "He's dead." I hear Quinn's voice in my head, but nothing can stop the fear in my body that he will show up.

My whole body starts to shake, and I look up at Shirley. "I'm going to be sick," I say, and she springs into action, grabbing a steel basin from under my bed and putting it in front of me as I vomit.

The pain rips through me as I shake so much my teeth are clattering. A warm hand rubs my back, and when I look up, I'm expecting it to be Shirley, but it's not. His blue eyes look straight into mine. I'm about to tell him I'm fine when Shirley comes back with a wet hand towel and puts it behind my neck.

I close my eyes, trying to catch my breath. "Take a sip of this," Quinn says, and I open my eyes to see him holding a cup of water in his hand. "It should make you feel better."

"Thank you," I mumble as Shirley takes the bowl away from me.

I take a deep breath. "I'm good. It was just," I say and then I stop talking. "Must be the motion of moving the bed."

"Must be," Quinn says, and just from his tone, I know he doesn't believe me. He looks at me, brushing the hair away from my forehead. "Drink a couple more sips of water," he says, his eyes never leaving mine. The thumping in my chest is starting to calm down.

Shirley clears her throat, making Quinn look over at her as he steps away from me. "We'll get you all cleaned up in a second," Shirley says as she pushes me down the hallway. I close my eyes and just feel myself being wheeled down the hallway.

I open my eyes when the light becomes a little bit darker and see I'm in the X-ray room. "Okay," Shirley says, locking the wheels on the bed. "Let's get these covers off you."

I look at her and then look at Quinn, who stands there and watches everything. "I'm okay," I say softly, and his eyes go just a touch lighter.

"Here we are," Shirley says as she slowly takes the cover off my legs, making sure that my hospital gown is in place.

I look down, seeing it pulled up more on one side. The sounds of hisses fills the room, and I look up at Quinn, who turns around. "I'll be outside," he says, pushing through the doors.

I look back down at the side of my leg, seeing my whole upper thigh a deep purple, the insides of the bruise turning blue. My hand flies out as I pull the gown down and look up at Shirley, whose eyes are filled with tears as she blinks them away and pretends that everything is okay. "In a couple of days, the color will fade," I mumble to her.

"Let's get you covered," she says, and then I have clean sheets on me in record time. "We are going to lower the bed," she tells me everything as she's doing it, making me relax just a touch more.

I close my eyes as the machine comes down, and she walks out of the room to take the X-ray. "All done."

"What next?" I ask as she unlocks the wheels and pushes me toward the doors.

"The doctor is going to get the images and then let us know," Shirley says, quietly pushing through the doors, and I see Quinn standing there with his back to the wall.

I avoid looking in his eyes. Instead, I close my eyes as she wheels me toward my room. "Can she eat?" Quinn asks Shirley, and I open my eyes.

"It depends on what is in that bag today," she says, shaking her head.

I watch Quinn look at her and smile shyly, and I look back at the brown bag. "She sent something for you, too," he says, and I look over at Shirley, who raises her eyebrows.

"What are you talking about?" I ask them, looking back and forth.

"My grandmother," Quinn says, going over to the brown bag and bringing it to me. "She likes to cook and bake." He looks at me, and his blue eyes shine when he talks about her. "She especially cooks and bakes when she is nervous. She's been on edge since everything went down." He puts the bag down, and I swear the bed dips. "So she sent a couple of things for you."

"For me?" I ask him, putting my hand to my chest. There has been no one in my whole life that has ever done anything for me.

"Well, yeah," he answers like it's a normal fucking thing. "Obviously."

The tears sting my eyes, and I have to swallow down the lump forming in my throat. This whole thing is just too much for me. "Did she pack some apple pie?" Shirley asks. He reaches into the bag and takes out container after container.

I look down at my legs, seeing all of the containers spread out on my bed. So many containers, he has to leave some in the bag. "Is that blueberry?" I ask when my eyes spot the purple in one of the containers.

"Yes." He nods, grabbing it. "It's my favorite," he says and looks at Shirley. "Can she?"

"Maybe just a touch," Shirley says. "You need to start with liquids first." She is about to say something else when the doctor comes into the room.

"Pie?" he asks, looking at the containers. "Pecan."

"She packed it especially for you," Quinn says, handing him the container. "For taking care of Willow."

My head spins as I take in the words. Why would she do that? My heart starts to speed up. "What is the verdict?" Shirley looks at the doctor.

"Looks like you were right," he says, looking at Shirley. "Her clavicle is broken."

"Her clavicle," Quinn says, shocked. "She's had a broken clavicle for the past four days, and no one knew?" His voice rises a bit, and then he looks at me. "Fine, my ass," he says and walks out of the room.

"What just happened?" I look at Shirley.

"That is him trying to show you that he's not a horse's ass," Shirley says, and I look out the window and watch him look up at the ceiling with his hands on his hips. "You should have seen him three days ago."

Nine

QUINN

I walk out of the room with my heart in my throat. My hands shake, and the anger and rage roar through me. If I would have stayed in the room, I don't know what I would have done or said. Neither of which would have boded well for anyone. I run my hands through my hair and then hold them behind my head.

Walking down the hall before and seeing her shaking like a leaf while she threw up was as if someone was pushing me to the edge of a cliff.

I tried to reel it in as I rubbed her back. I couldn't tell her that she was going to be okay; I didn't trust any words to come out of my mouth, so I kept silent beside her as Shirley made sure she was okay. It was going as well as it could have gone, but then I saw that her whole fucking leg was bruised. Not just one spot, either. Her whole fucking upper leg was bruised a dark purple. It screamed at me that this wasn't just one punch that created that. I closed my eyes, trying not to see it, but it was the only thing I saw in my mind.

I had to walk out of the room because I thought I was going to be sick in the middle of the hallway. Knowing someone put their hands on her, I felt this rage soar through me, and I had no idea what the fuck was going on inside me. All I wanted to do was push the hair back from her face, just stare into her eyes, and hold her face in my palms. I wanted to take her in my arms and promise her that she would never be hurt again. I wanted to tell her that I would die before I let someone else put their hands on her. Then hearing that she had a broken clavicle and just fought through the pain? Well, that was the push I needed to go over the edge.

I put my hands on the nurses' desk and look up at the ceiling, trying to calm myself. I make the mistake of looking over my shoulder at her as she looks down at her lap, probably unsure as to what the fuck happened.

"Well, that was smooth," Shirley says. Coming out, she shakes her head and gives me the biggest glare ever. "Idiot." I can't even say anything to that because she is right. I have no idea what's come over me, but I'm in uncharted territory, so I have no idea how to act. "I'm going to get her a sling for her arm." She turns and walks down the hall while the doctor comes out with his pecan pie in his hand.

"She'll be fine," he says. "It's a common injury."

"Really? How many adults do you know that come in with a broken clavicle?" I ask, my eyes staring straight at him.

"A lot more than you think," he says, and I tilt my head to the side, not believing him for even a second. "It could happen riding a bike or playing sports." He tries to sugarcoat things. "Car accidents."

"Or from being almost beaten to death," I add, and he doesn't correct me. "How long will it take to heal?"

"Usually, it takes six to eight weeks to heal in adults. With her arm in a sling, she won't be in much pain," he says. "I'll check in with her later." He turns to walk away, and I start to take a step into the room when I see Shirley coming back.

"How about you calm down a touch and then come in?"

she says. "This might hurt, and she might not show it in front of you."

I nod at her as she walks in, and I hear her talking, the phone in my back pocket buzzing. Looking at it, I see it's my uncle Jacob. "Hello," I say, my eyes never leaving from looking into the window at Shirley explaining to Willow what she is going to be doing.

"Quinn," he says. "I'm with the guys. You are on speakerphone."

"Okay," I say, confused. I step down the hall, looking into the room where Chelsea was and see it's empty. The hospital bed sits ready for the next patient. I turn back as I slowly walk back to Willow's room.

"I hate to do this to you," he says, and I'm already annoyed. I don't even ask him what guys he has there. Is he with my father, or is he with his men at the station? Either way, I couldn't care less.

"I'm going to be honest," I start to say. "It's not a good time," I say instead of saying what I want to say, which is I don't want to hear it.

"Well, sorry, but we are running out of time at this point," he says, and I stand straight. "We need to come in and interview her."

"No," I say right away. "Fuck no." My voice goes low as I hiss it out.

"We've given her more time than anyone else," he says, and I close my eyes. "We haven't even placed an officer outside of her room."

I ignore that last point. "She literally woke up yesterday," I say. "Less than twenty-four hours ago. She was in a coma for four days. When would you have asked her questions exactly?"

"And we should have had someone there get a statement." His voice comes in. "But we gave her some time because of you." His voice trails off, and I know that he's bent many rules because of me being by Willow's side.

"Well, you aren't coming today," I say, my voice a touch louder. "She just got results back, and her clavicle is broken." My voice trails off with that statement.

"What?" he whispers.

"Yeah," I say. "She was fighting through the pain and not saying anything, but I guess the nurse saw it, and she just got the results."

"Okay, fine," he huffs. "We'll be there tomorrow afternoon. That is the longest I can stretch it. There are lots of loose ends to this investigation, and we hope she can help us."

"Yeah," I say, looking into the room at her, knowing that she holds many answers. "Okay, I'll text you tomorrow morning to set up a time." I finally give in.

"Hang in there," Jacob says. "It's almost over."

I disconnect the call. "Or it's just beginning," I mumble to myself. Putting the phone back in my back pocket, I rub my face with my hands as I watch Shirley talk to Willow.

I watch as Shirley explains something to her. Willow looks at Shirley and smiles softly at her, and she is breathtakingly beautiful. Shirley bends Willow's arm, putting it in the bottom part of the sling. Willow winces just a bit when she sits up in the bed so Shirley can slip it around the bottom of her chest. Willow slowly puts her back against the bed and listens to whatever Shirley tells her. She leans her head back against the pillow. Her eyes close just for a second, and then she fights to open them again.

You can see that she is fighting the sleep that will take her soon. I just stand here and watch. Shirley takes the containers off the bed, putting them back into the brown bag, but keeping out the blueberry one. She stays in the room, not leaving her side until she falls asleep.

She walks out of the room, coming to my side in front of

the window that looks in. "I guess it was too much excitement for her," she says, looking at her watch. "It's the longest she's been up." I nod, looking at her chest rising and falling. "She's out for a couple of hours. I just gave her another dose of pain medication."

"How much pain was she in?" I look over at Shirley. "And she didn't say anything?" I watch her face as she talks, seeing if she'll hide anything from me.

"Everyone has their own threshold for pain," she says matter-of-factly. "We all handle it differently." She stands in front of me, her eyes not giving away anything. I turn back and watch Willow. "Why don't you take off for a couple of hours?" I side-eye her. "It might be what you need. Get out of here and get a good night's sleep. She isn't going anywhere," she says, and I just shake my head.

"That woman"—she points at Willow—"has been through more than we will ever know. More than she will ever admit to anyone." She swallows down the lump in her throat. "I want you to keep that in mind when you talk to her." I ignore the beating of my own heart, and the way my stomach sinks at her words.

"They need to come and get an official statement from her tomorrow afternoon," I say, and she shakes her head.

"That is going to be interesting," she says. "Will you be in the room?"

"What do you think?" I cross my arms over my chest.

"I don't think that is a good idea," she answers honestly. I just look over at her. "I don't know you, Quinn," she starts, looking at me over her glasses that sit on the tip of her nose, "but from what I can tell, I don't think you can listen to her story without losing your shit." I almost roll my eyes at her. "Think about that before tomorrow. She is going to need someone on her side." She takes a deep breath. "And I don't think anyone has ever been on her side."

I don't answer because she turns around and walks away from me to the nurses' desk. She sits there and writes in the folder. I walk back into the room and go to sit in the chair beside Willow's bed. Shirley's words replay in my head. *"And I don't think anyone has ever been on her side."*

I watch her sleep, and she whimpers. I scoot forward and hold her hand in mine, the casted arm in the sling. Her eyes open halfway. "I'm here," I tell her as she blinks, trying to stay awake.

"Does it hurt?" I whisper.

She licks her lips. "Not really." She closes her eyes.

"I'm sorry about before," I say, not sure if she is awake or not. "I should have held your hand while you went through all of that." Her eyes flutter open just for a second before closing again.

Her eyes open again. "You don't have to be sorry," she says softly. "You didn't do anything to hurt me." Her voice trails off, and then she closes them again, this time not opening them as she slips back to sleep.

"Tomorrow is going to be tough," I say when the sun goes down, the hallway gets dark, and she still hasn't woken up. I put her small hand in mine as I trail my finger on the top of her hand. "But I'm going to be here," I say. She mumbles as her fingers twitch in my hand. "I'm going to be here, and I'm going to be by your side."

Ten

WILLOW

"I'm going to be by your side." I hear his soft voice, and I fight to open my eyes, I feel the softness on my hand, but the heaviness stops me as I sink into sleep again. I want to force my eyes open again to talk to him.

I'm in the dark forest as I hear his voice over and over again. "You will never be free of me," he says as I run away from the voice. Running as fast as I can, I fall over the rocks. The pain rips through me, and I scream, my eyes flying open, and I look around the dark room.

I blink a couple of times, this time getting my eyes adjusted, the lights from the nurses' station coming in just a bit. Enough for me to see around the room just a touch. The room is unchanged from the last time, the containers of pie still sitting uneaten on the shelf.

My body aches suddenly. I have been sore before in my life, but nothing like this. My whole body screams out every single time I try to move.

My arm presses down on my chest. The sling is tied tightly around my waist. The pain in my shoulder is just a fraction of what it was yesterday.

My hand warms as I look down and see Quinn with his head on the bed, right next to his hand on top of mine. I think about moving my hand, but I don't want to wake him.

When the doctor came into the room yesterday to tell me that my clavicle was broken, the first thing I did was look over at Quinn, whose face went from a smile to rage. I tried not to watch him walk out of the room. I tried to pretend it didn't bother me. I pretended I didn't care. I shouldn't care, I kept reminding myself.

I look down at this man who I don't think has slept since I came here. I have never seen him with his guard down, but I get to look at him for once, without him looking back at me. I get to see the softness of his face. I get to see the way his hair falls softly on his forehead. I wonder if his hair feels like silk.

Who the hell is this man? I have so many questions about him and no way to find out. The only way I can find out is if he tells me, and I'm not going to ask him. Because I know if I ask him the question, I have to be ready to answer his questions, and I don't know how to do that without baring my whole fucking soul.

He must sense I'm watching him because his eyes blink open for a second and then close again, only for a couple of seconds before he blinks again as he looks up at me staring at him.

He gets up, groaning when he rolls his neck. "Did I wake you?" he asks softly.

"What are you still doing here?" I ask, and he looks at me with a confused look. "Who are you really?"

His voice comes out almost in a whisper. "I can ask you the same," he says, and I swallow down the lump in my throat that comes out.

"I don't know what you mean," I say and avoid his eyes. "I'm no one." I blink away the tears that threaten to fall. I blink as fast as I can to fight them away.

"You are not no one," he says, his eyes hard. "I don't know your story, and I'm not sure you'll actually tell me, but one thing I know for sure is that you are not no one." He looks down at his hand on top of mine, and he slowly moves it off. The cold air hits my hand as soon as it's free from his. He sits back in the chair. "Do you want water?" he asks as if he just didn't stop my heart in my throat.

He walks out of the room, and only then do I let a tear escape, wiping it away as soon as I feel it on my cheek. "He didn't mean it," I tell myself. "He doesn't know you."

He comes back into the room with a cup in his hand. "Do you want me to open the shades?" He holds the cup in his hand and holds it for me. "The sun is almost set to rise."

The cold water feels refreshing when I take a couple of sips. "I take it you're a morning person?"

He smiles and chuckles. "You can say that." He puts the cup down, walks over to the shades, and opens them. The sky is still dark, but you can see that the sun is about to rise.

"Do you watch the sun rise every day?" I don't know why I'm asking him.

"Pretty much," he says, looking out the window. "I get up at around five."

"Why?" I say before I can stop myself.

"I guess my body is just used to it," he says, and I want to know why. "My mother said I was the worst sleeper out of all of us."

"All of you?" I ask, intrigued by his statement.

"I have a brother, Reed, who is two years younger than me, and my sister, Harlow, who is five years younger than me." His whole face lights up when he talks about his family. "Do you have any siblings?"

"No," I say, shaking my head, and I don't add the thank God.

I don't say anything else because he looks back out of the

61

window. For the first time in my life, I watch the sun rise without having the fear that I don't know where I will be that night. For the first time, I don't have to wonder if he is going to be in a good mood or not. For the first time, I watch the sun rise without hating the fact that I'm alive.

The yellow sun slowly takes over the whole sky, and for the first time in my life, I wish I was outside to feel the heat on my face. I close my eyes as the sun shines in the window. "Maybe soon," Quinn says. "We can see if we can watch the sunrise outside."

"Why do you like watching it?" I ask him.

"It's almost therapeutic." With a smirk, he grabs a container of pie and comes over to me. "It's like a restart."

"That makes no sense." I shake my head.

He smiles at me. "It makes all the sense in the world." He opens the container of pie. "Let's say today is one of the worst days you've ever had." He starts to talk. "And the only thing you can think of is I can't wait for this day to be over. You ever have those days?"

I laugh. "I was left for dead. So chances are, I've had more than a few of those days." I try to make a joke of it, but I can see his eyes go dark. I see his Adam's apple move as he swallows.

"The sunrise shows you that today is another day. It shows you that you have a reset." He smiles and puts the pie in my lap, and I look down, seeing it's blueberry.

I look down at the pie, my mouth watering. "You ever see the glass half empty?" I ask him, my hand itching to grab the plastic spoon he holds in his hand.

"Do you ever see the glass half full?" he counters and extends his hand with the spoon. "You just have to have a bit of faith."

I hold up my hand and reach for the spoon. "In my life ..." He holds on to the spoon. "I learned early on that faith wasn't on my side." His eyes are on mine. "I learned that in my life when I thought the glass was half full, it was quickly shown to me that not only was it not half full but it was, in fact, empty. A figment of my imagination at times." I look at the spoon in my hand and then the pie. "See this pie." I put the spoon down on my lap and pick up the container. "What do you see?"

"I see a piece of pie," he says, and I look down and blink away the tears that are fighting to be let out.

"I see a piece of pie also," I tell him, smiling and then looking back at the pie. "But I also see something that will give me a little bit of joy because it's my favorite. But then I see something that can be used to make me feel disappointment." His mouth opens. "You see, if I show even a bit of emotion toward this piece of pie, it gives someone, anyone, the chance to use it against me." I try to shrug my shoulders. "It's the way the world works for me."

I watch him as he takes in the words I've just said. I watch him as he struggles with not flying off the handle. I watch his hands clench into fists on his legs and then I see them open as he rubs up and down his upper thighs. "Eat the pie," he says through clenched teeth.

"I can't eat much," I say. "I haven't eaten in eight days," I say, and he looks at me.

"You mean six days," he corrects me.

I shake my head. "No, I mean eight days." His jaw goes tight. "And experience reminds me that if I eat this whole thing, it'll be wasted because my stomach will most likely throw most of it up." I pick up the spoon. "So I'm going to have two bites." I cut a piece and bring it to my lips. "It smells so good," I say.

"When you get out of here," he says, getting up and smiling at me, "I'm going to take you to my grandmother's house." My heart speeds up in my chest. "She's going to bake it in front of you, and then, Willow," he whispers, "you are going to eat the whole fucking pie." He walks away from my bed. "I'm going to tell them you're awake."

I don't say anything to him as I watch him walk out of the room and then look down at the pie with the tears I lost the battle against. They roll down my cheeks as I try not to sob out. I take a bite of the pie and let the sweetness sit on my tongue. My whole mouth waters at the same time as I chew the little bite. After the second bite, I put the spoon down. Looking out at the nurses' station, I see him with his head down and his arms outstretched to his sides; hands that look so strong. Hands that look like they will hold you up instead of push you down.

"You will never be good enough for anyone." I hear the voice in the back of my head. The voice so many times, hurting me more and more. "The sooner you admit it to yourself." I hear her voice again. "The better it will be for everyone."

I close my eyes, trying not to make her words hurt me. She is nothing to you. All I can do is hear her laughing in the background just like she always does. "The apple doesn't fall far from the tree."

My eyes fly open as I try to run away from her voice, my heart speeding up as I push her back in the black box I buried her in. "I hope you are rotting in hell," I mumble. "Burning in hell."

Eleven

QUINN

I stand in front of the nurses' station with my hands by my sides, trying to make the burning in my stomach go away. I made a note that she is going to have blueberry fucking pie every single day that I'm here. Every fucking day that I'm around her.

"Good morning," Shirley says, coming out from another room. "Is she up?"

"She is," I say. "She is going to have two bites of pie."

"I'll see if we have something for her for breakfast," she says, "and she is expected to go for tests this morning." I look at her, and the worry must show all over my face. "Routine tests. We need to see if the swelling in her head has gone down."

"Okay," I say quietly and turn to walk back into the room. I see her with her eyes closed as one tear rolls down her cheek. "Are you okay?"

"Who are you, Quinn?" She opens her eyes, and I see they are filled with tears. "I can't pinpoint who you are." My heart speeds up as I walk over to the chair and sit down next to her bed. I want to get closer to the bed and hold her hand in mine.

"My head keeps going around and around in circles as I think about who you really are."

"Who do you think I am?" I ask, trying to get her to talk to me and open up a bit more. My hands get clammy as I ask her the loaded question.

"That is the problem," she says, and I notice that her index finger taps the bed. Something she does when she's nervous. "It's a toss-up." We stare at each other, both of us unwilling to look away. "Between a cop or a therapist."

My laughter fills the room. "Why do you think I'm a cop?" I lean back in the chair, putting my hands on my stomach as I watch her.

"For one, the way you ask me questions indirectly," she says right away. "You dance around a lot, trying to get me to say something without you saying it."

"Is that because you have been arrested or questioned in the past that you know that?" I watch her eyes get just a touch darker.

"Not that it's on the record," she admits and waits for me to answer her.

"Okay," I tell her. "I'm not a cop. But," I say, putting up my index finger, "my uncle Jacob is a sheriff, and well, he's been my role model since I can remember. I spent a lot of summers trailing him. Much to my mother's begging."

"She didn't want you to be a sheriff?" she asks, and I chuckle.

"She didn't want her child to be hurt," I say, and her next words slice me through the heart.

"Be happy. Not all mothers are like that." She swallows. "Trust me, I know." I want to ask her what she means, but I know for her to open up to me, she has to trust me, and talking to her will help. "So you're a therapist, then?" she asks, and I shake my head.

"Not exactly," I say, not sure I should be happy she guessed it. "But close."

"What does that mean?" she asks me, confused.

"I run Barnes Therapy Program," I say, smiling.

"What is that?" she asks, her eyes waiting for my answer.

"It's an equine therapy farm," I say and see her eyebrows pinch together. "It's horse therapy." She opens her mouth. "I started it when I turned twenty," I say, describing my baby to her. "With two horses. Initially, it started with soldiers who would come home with PTSD symptoms. They would come by every day and do a couple of hours with the horse. Then we expanded it to women who come from abusive homes." I see the flicker in her eyes. "It's a different approach to healing."

"So they ride the horses?" she asks.

"Oh, there are a lot of things to do before you ride the horse." She tilts her head. "You have to gain the horse's trust. But yes, eventually, you work your way up to that," I say. "I started with two horses, and I'm up to twenty, and I have a waiting list a mile long." I don't tell her that I have three centers, and one is about to become a rehab for soldiers who come back home.

"It helps?" she asks, and I can see she wants to ask me more questions.

"It helps because you have to be calm and relaxed with the horse. Most of my horses are also rescue horses."

"So you just like to save everything and anyone that is broken?" She laughs.

"Not everything," I say. "But I definitely relate more to horses than I do to people."

"I mean, your bedside manner," she says, "could use some help." She laughs, and it's the best sound I've heard in my whole life.

"Is that so?" I'm about to say something else when Shirley comes in.

"Did I just hear someone laughing?" Shirley walks into the room holding a tray in her hand, looking at me and then Willow, who has a smile on her face. "I don't think I've ever heard you laugh before."

"I don't usually have anything to laugh about," Willow says, looking over at her. "Is that my breakfast?"

"It is." Shirley sets the hospital tray down on the table. "Now, don't get your hopes up too high," Shirley says. "We have to wean you into solid foods."

"I know," she says. "Besides, I had two bites of blueberry pie."

"Did you now?" She smiles at her. "Well, eat up because I have to draw your blood, and then we have a CT scan and an MRI."

"Why?" she asks.

"We want to make sure that the swelling in your brain went down," Shirley says. "Make sure you are healing. They are totally normal."

"Okay," she answers softly, her head going back on the pillow as she closes her eyes.

"Are you hungry?" I ask, and she shakes her head.

"Not really." She closes her eyes a touch more.

"Rest, sweet girl," Shirley says, and Willow's eyes close and don't open again. Shirley motions with her head for me to follow her out of the room.

"Is she okay?" I ask, worried. Looking over my shoulder, I make sure she is still sleeping.

"She is fine," she says. "Does she know about this afternoon?"

I shake my head. "I haven't told her yet," I say, running my hand through my hair. "She was light and laughing, and I didn't want to."

"You better get your balls ready because in less than five hours, that woman is going to be raked over the coals." She points at the room. "And there is nothing that anyone can do about it."

She turns to walk away, leaving me with a nagging feeling in my stomach. The burning takes over, and it moves up my neck, my mouth getting drier. My legs feel like I have concrete in my shoes as I walk back into the room and sit in the chair by her bed.

Her face has gained color in the past couple of days, and the circles around her eyes have gotten lighter. The swelling on one side has gone down just a touch. The sound of her laughter echoes in my ears, and I want to hear it again. Over and over again.

I take my phone out and send my father a text.

Me: What time is everyone coming?

I watch as the bubble with three dots comes up and see that it's just after seven. It doesn't surprise me that he's awake. My father might sit behind a desk most of the day, but he always starts his day at five thirty with a walk to the barn.

Dad: We are going to be there at one.

Me: Can you bring blueberry pie?

Dad: Yeah, I'll get one on my way there. Are you okay?

Me: No. Not even close.

Dad: It'll be fine. Have faith.

I put the phone down and roll my eyes. My phone beeps again.

Dad: Don't roll your eyes at me. I can still kick your ass.

I laugh, and it wakes her up. She jumps, gasping out for air. "It's fine," I say, grabbing her hand that is shaking in mine. "It's fine." Her chest rises and falls, and the machine shows her heart going higher than before but coming down just a touch. "It was a nightmare." I rub my thumb over the top of her hand. "It's just a nightmare."

"Sometimes, your nightmares are reality," she says, licking her lips. "I've found that out way too many times."

"Not anymore." I wait for her to look at me. "Nothing will ever hurt you again."

Her eyes drop to look at our hands, and I can feel her trying to come up with something else. "Willow, look at me." Her eyes come back to me. "You never ever have to feel fear again." My thumb rubs across her hand softly. Her eyes go from my eyes to my hand on her and then up to the ceiling, and I know I have to tell her. "Um," I start to say, and she looks at me. "I'm sorry to have to do this to you." Her eyes never leave mine. "But they need to come and get a statement." I swallow. "I tried to push it off as long as I could, but …"

"It's fine," she says, moving her hand away from mine. "It's been long enough."

"Do you want me to get a lawyer for you?" I ask, and I hold my breath.

"No," she says. "I did nothing wrong."

"I'll be here the whole time," I tell her, and Shirley enters.

"Okay, you ready to go?" she asks Willow, who avoids our eyes by closing hers. "It should be a couple of hours." She looks at me, and I just nod.

I walk over to the window and look outside at the sun slowly waking up. I stand here looking out for I don't know how long, until Shirley comes back with her, and Willow has her eyes closed.

"She had a headache," Shirley says. "She couldn't open her eyes without having sharp pain, so we gave her something."

"How long will she be out?" I ask as she locks her bed wheels.

"Shouldn't be long," she says. "But she was very quiet." I nod at her, and she walks out of the room.

I sit in the chair and watch her sleep. Her head moves side to side, and then her eyes fly open, and she closes them right away. I get up, going over to the blinds, and close them. "See if this is better."

She opens her eyes slowly, nodding her head. I don't have time to tell her anything because there is a knock on the door.

I look over and see my father standing there, wearing dress pants and a button-down shirt rolled at the sleeves. "Hi," he says, and I look over at Willow, who looks at my father and then at me.

"Willow, this is my father, Casey," I say, and my father walks over to her and smiles.

"Willow, good to meet you," he says.

There is another knock on the door, and I look up to see my uncle Jacob and uncle Beau. "Hey," they both say, coming into the room. Willow's eyes go from one to the other as she tries to figure out who everyone is.

"This is my uncle Jacob," I say, pointing at my uncle, and I see in her eyes that she recognizes the name. "Then my uncle Beau."

They smile at her, and then another knock makes us look at the door. I look over at the same time as Willow, and then she screams.

My head turns in slow motion. Everyone in the room turns to look at Willow, who is shaking in the middle of the bed. "Oh my God," she says, trying to move out of the bed. I get to the side of the bed as she tries to get as far away as she can. "He's here."

Twelve

WILLOW

My body shakes, and I can't even stop it, the sound of my heart pounding out of my chest. I try to turn and escape off the bed when Quinn puts his hands around me. "It's okay." His heat from his hand soaks right through my hospital gown, and I look up at him. His soft blue eyes calm something inside me. "Promise." I don't know why, but something in the way he says those words, I believe him.

"I'm not my father." The man speaks, and I turn to look at him, finally taking in his appearance. His body is much bigger than his father's, his eyes just a touch lighter. His face not sunken in and filled with hatred.

"I'm Mayson," he says, and I let go just a bit and sink back into the bed.

I look at Quinn, who just nods his head, telling me that what this man is saying is the truth. "What are you all doing here?" I ask, my voice trembling as I look at all the men standing in my room.

"We have questions for you," Quinn's father, Casey, says. They look the same and could be brothers. His father has a bit of white at his temples, and Quinn is a bit wider than his father, but everything down to their eyes is the same.

"I thought I was talking to the sheriff," I say, looking at Jacob. Sitting in the middle of the bed, I feel my mouth suddenly dry as my hands shake. I sink back into the warmth of the bed, hoping that it spreads through my body.

"You will be," Jacob says, and Quinn walks over to the table. I want to yell at him not to leave me. I want to tell him that I want him beside me, but I just let him go. "The investigation has been ongoing, and lots of people have been working on it. I hope this is okay?" Quinn grabs the white cup and brings it over to me.

I ignore the cup of water that Quinn holds in his hand, refusing to give them any leverage over me. "What do you want to know?" I look at all of them, and my eyes go to Mayson as he stares at me. I wonder if he knows what I went through. I wonder if he can tell the hell I've lived in. I wonder if he knew all this time and ignored it.

"Who are you?" Mayson asks before anyone else.

"My name is Rosemary Davis." I give them my full legal name. I look at their faces and see that they have never heard of me, which means I covered my tracks. "But I was always crying as a child, so they called me weeping Willow instead."

"When did you meet my father?" Mayson asks.

"Lucifer?" I say the name that I gave him, and Mayson just smirks at me. "I met him eight years ago."

"How?" Jacob asks, watching my every move.

"My mother was married to him," I admit, and I see the surprise on their faces. "He was her fifth husband. She really did save the best for last."

"That's impossible," Casey says. "We would have found that Rosalie had a child in her background check. There were no family members, just a mother."

I laugh bitterly. "She had me when she was fifteen years

old. She was trouble even then. I have no idea who my father is. I don't think she knew either. Needless to say, she didn't want me. She was too young to take care of herself, let alone have a child." I fill them in. "My grandmother, Louise, she put her name on my birth certificate as my mother." I swallow the lump in my throat as I remember her gentle smile. If I close my eyes tight enough, I can still hear her voice very far away.

"Rosalie had me at home, so there was no one to say otherwise. But who knows if any of that is true. When I was seven, my grandmother, who was my mother in everyway, was killed in a car accident driving home from the grocery store while I was at school. I was placed with child protective services." I wipe the tear off my face. "Until Rosalie showed up at the funeral. She was half stoned out of her mind and let everyone know she was my real mother." The white cup in Quinn's hand is crushed, and I look over at him as he puts his head down. He probably is disgusted by me, I think, ignoring how the pain in my chest comes on full force. "We had no other family members, so Rosalie had no one to fight to keep me." I tap my finger on the bed. "She didn't want me. She wanted the inheritance I came with." I look at them. "And then when she died two years ago, I was stuck with Benjamin." I say his real name, and the bile comes up in my throat.

"How did you live with them and no one ever heard of you?" Casey asks. "We interviewed them."

I laugh. "Those people wouldn't know the queen if she stayed with us." I look down. "The longest we stayed in one place was four months. My mother followed her 'one true love.'" I use my hands to make quotation marks around the saying she used to always use. "Then we met Benjamin, and I wasn't really allowed out." I don't give any more information than I need to.

"What does that mean?" Quinn asks.

"I was a pawn in their game," I finally say. It's the only thing I can say truthfully.

"What does that mean?" Mayson asks.

"It means that if I didn't do what one person wanted, they would get the other person to persuade me to do it. No matter what it took." It's the easiest way I can explain it at this point. I don't tell them just how far they took it. I don't tell them that the longest I went without eating was twelve days. They would hydrate me but use food as leverage. I don't tell them any of the bad stories. That is my nightmare to live with. "All that changed when Rosalie died. Then I was his to do what he pleased with. There were no more games." I look at Mayson. "When he found you, it was like he climbed Everest, and nothing was going to stop him from making sure you paid for what you did to him."

"Were you there when he held me captive?" Mayson asks with his eyes on me.

"I was there," I say, and he glares at me. "Tied and bound." His eyes soften. "I tried to get free and get you help," I inform him. "I waited for him to fall asleep one night. Fall into a stupor after drinking his whiskey. I waited until I knew he was passed out before I made my move. I was going to untie you, but when I was about to pull the door open, the floor creaked. I didn't have time to look behind me to see that he was awake. In the darkness like the devil he was, he grabbed my hair, pulling it out, and rammed my head into the wall."

I look at Mayson. "When you escaped? God, that was a good day." I smile at him, not even feeling the tears streaming down my face. "I laughed at him." I shake my head. "Which, if you haven't figured out, he doesn't like too much. He back-handed me, and something in me snapped, and all I could do was laugh at him. I think it was hysteria. I don't even know how long the beating lasted. I don't know what happened after that because everything went black, and when I woke up, we were in the car, and it was two weeks later." I ignore the gasp that fills the room. "I was in and out for most of the time. I don't really remember much. He had to keep a low profile, so we slept in the car."

"Were you there when he followed Chelsea?" Mayson asks me. "Outside the diner."

"I was." I look at Jacob. "I was in the getaway car, handcuffed to the steering wheel. He had the keys. He came running back, started the car, and told me to go." My finger taps the bed faster and faster. "I refused. I was done with it." I force myself not to cry. He will not get any more tears from me. "I didn't care."

"But you drove away?" Jacob says.

"Yes, well, when you have a gun pointed at your head, you pretty much listen." I look down. "I didn't actually. I told him no, and he pulled the trigger, then he laughed and said, 'Let's play Russian roulette.'" The same fear runs through me. "So I took off instead of finding out if I would be lucky again. The sound of the gun clicking right next to your ear is a sound you will never ever forget."

"How much longer is this going to take?" Quinn asks, and when I look back at him, I see the rage on his face. "Ask your questions, and let's get this over with. She needs rest."

"I have a couple more questions," Jacob says. "Where were you when he kidnapped Chelsea?"

"I was unconscious under a bed," I tell them. "I tried to warn you again. I should have learned my lesson, but he was going to kill her. There was no mistake. He was obsessed with making sure Mayson suffered hell. You"—I look at Mayson —"were his kryptonite. For as long as I can remember, it was Mayson, the one who fucked him over. Mayson is the only one who was able to escape him and his wrath." I take another deep breath.

"I thought he was gone. I opened the door and took five

steps before he stepped out and found me. I begged him to kill me. I said whatever I could to make him mad enough to give me the last final blow." My hands shake. "Called him a loser. Called him a misfit. Called him a sorry excuse of a man. What kind of man makes his son win. I said everything and anything I could in order for him to kill me. With each blow, I laughed in his face. His blows would get harder and harder until I was numb. Until I was just a corpse in the middle of that smelly cabin. I don't remember anything until Quinn found me."

I look over at Quinn, whose face is white and ashen. "I'll be back," he says, turning and walking out of the room. I look at his father, who follows him out.

"I don't know what else you need me to answer," I say to the men who are left in the room. My heart beats a mile a minute. "He killed my mother and kept me because I got a check every month. He didn't keep me because he loved me or was taking care of me. I was living in hell, and he was the gatekeeper."

"No one wants you. You are nothing, a nobody. No one would care if you died or lived," I hear echoed in my ears. I close my eyes, trying to drown out the laughing that would come after that. I open my eyes and look out the window at Quinn, who has his back to me.

My heart feels this weird pressure in my chest, knowing what I said might have hurt him. I've never had anyone sit by my bed before and worry about me. I've never had anyone care that I was hurt. I've never had anyone give me even an ounce of what he gave me in the little time he's known me. I don't even know him, yet I know that if he's here, I'll be safe.

Thirteen

QUINN

I walk out of the room, and my whole body shakes with rage. My stomach burns, and I have the sudden need to throw up. I listened to her tell her story, and I knew it wasn't going to be pretty. I knew it would be a hard one, but what I didn't realize was that she spent her whole fucking life in hell.

"You need to rein it in," my father says from behind me. I know I can't turn around because if I do, she will see my face and the horror on it. She will see the tears running down my face. She will see that, and then she will spin it to something else. I know her, in the short time, I know her.

"Dad," I whisper or plead, even I don't know. "I can't." I swallow down the lump forming in my throat. My head is spinning around and around as I replay the words. "So many things make sense. The way she didn't want to ask for a thing or admit she needed things, like fucking water."

"You need to," he says and walks over to stand in front of me. "There are so many holes in her story it's not funny. And frankly"—he shakes his head—"I'm not sure I want to know them. But for her, for right now, you need to be strong."

"I can tell you what isn't in those stories." I look at him.

"There is no one tucking her in at night and telling her good night. There is no one telling her that they love her. No one kissing her when she got hurt. No one protecting her. No one." My voice drops to a whisper. "She had none of that." My heart shatters when I get the full picture.

"I know," he says. "Trust me, I know, and I am going to be real with you right now. I don't even think we heard the worst of it."

I swallow down the bile coming up my throat. "It's a good thing that son of a bitch is dead," I say, my hands going to fists at my sides. "It's a good thing they're both dead because ..."

"I know," he says, slapping my shoulder with his hand and squeezing it. The love from him is apparent, love she never felt. "Now we need to get in there and listen to the rest of the story."

I nod and take a deep breath before turning around and walking back into the room. My eyes go to hers as she avoids looking at me. "Okay, if it's alright," Jacob says, "I'm going to just ask you some timeline questions. Just so we can clear up some things and make sure you weren't involved."

"You're kidding, right?" Mayson says with his hands on his hips.

"Isn't it enough?" I say, my voice not coming out as soft as I wanted it to. "Didn't you get everything you were looking for?"

"It's fine," Willow says. "But I have a question." I look at her and see she is afraid to ask it. "There was a black backpack."

"I have it," Mayson says. I can see her eyes fill with tears, but she blinks them away as fast as they come.

"Would I be able to get it back?" she asks and holds her breath.

"I'll bring it to you tonight," he says. She looks down, and I see a tear fall on her hand.

"You said that your mother met Benjamin," Jacob starts, and she nods.

"They met at a bar, I think, or a party. I have no idea," she says. "He came home one day and never left. They would get high together, drink together. I tried to stay out of sight. They let me go to school for a bit, but then, well, a teacher noticed the bruises and started to ask questions. They yanked me out and homeschooled me. I managed to do online classes and graduated at sixteen." I smile at her. Even with everything stacked against her, she managed to do all of that.

"Do you know when he changed his name?" he asks, and she nods.

"Oh, yeah," she says. "He had a roaring good time. Then the high left, and I couldn't find his new credit card, so he broke four of my fingers." She holds up her right hand. "I had to use popsicle sticks and tape to get them back to normal. Listen, I know you are trying to piece stuff together, and if you haven't figured it out, it wasn't good. Nothing in the last eight years was good." She sounds tired, tired and frustrated, and at the edge of a breakdown, but she refuses to let anyone see it.

"He would use my mother against me. If I didn't do what he wanted, he would hurt her. At first, I protected her." She looks down. "Then ..." She laughs as tears stream down her face. "Then she would sell me out. Tell him things I loved so he would keep them from me. Like water. Like a bed. Like food. Like a shower. They would dangle a simple shower in front of me until I gave in and gave them whatever it was that they wanted." She holds her head high. "Things were calm for two months. The credit cards would then be maxed out, and he would have no money until another one would come in. And then the rent was due, so we would have to be ready to move in the middle of the night."

"Your mother passed away," Jacob says, and I look at her.

"Rosalie is not my mother," she corrects him. "A mother

doesn't treat a child like that." I don't know if I can stand much longer. I look over at my father, who can feel that my strings are about to snap.

"When Rosalie passed away, where were you?" he asks, and I see her look down and then up again.

"I was unconscious in the corner of a motel room," she answers him. "They were going at it, I don't even know why anymore, and I told them that someone was going to call the cops." She shakes her head. "I knew it wasn't true. It was a run-down motel that rented rooms by the half hour. He back-handed me a couple of times, and then when I came to, he was sitting on the bed looking down at Rosalie. She was lying there with her eyes open, looking back at him." She puts her hand to her stomach, and her face goes as white as a ghost as she relives it. "He put her in the car and drove her to the hospital and dumped her there." She closes her eyes and moves her hand to put it on her head.

"This is over," I say, my voice coming out tight. The guys look over at me. "This is enough for one day." I look over at her and see that her head is down. I want to walk over to her, put my arm around her, and tell her she is so brave as I kiss her tears away from her cheeks.

"We've got enough." Mayson steps up. "We don't need anything else." He looks at me, and we share a silent look, then he turns back and looks at Willow. "I'll bring your bag."

She nods at him as he walks out of the room. Beau, who hasn't said a word this whole time, looks at me and then turns to Willow. "Thank you," he says, his voice soft, "for your courage."

She sniffles, looking down at her hand that is shaking. I step forward and hold it in my hand. It feels like ice. She side-looks at our hands together. "I have to say," Jacob says. "It's an ongoing investigation, so I have to tell you this next part." I look at him, and he looks at me and then at Willow. "You can't leave town."

She looks at him. "Where the hell am I going to go?"

"She's staying with me," I say out loud, and all eyes come to me. "When she is discharged, she'll be staying with me." I look at Willow, who just stares at me with her mouth open.

"Perfect," Jacob says. "If you remember anything else, let me know."

He looks at me and then walks out of the room. "Willow," my father says. "I'm sorry that you had to relive all of that."

"I know that you guys needed answers," she says. "You guys have to know that if I could have gotten you help, I would have."

"We know," he says, smiling at her. Walking out of the room, he grabs a brown bag. "Now, I don't know if you can eat yet or not, but ..." He puts it on the tray. "But my mother found out you like blueberry pie," he says and then takes the pie wrapped in hand towels out of the bag. "It was baked fresh this morning." He places it on the table and then unties the top of it.

"What do we have here?" Shirley says from the doorway, looking at us. "Is that blueberry?"

"It is," Willow says, looking at the pie. "She made it for me?" she asks, confused, and my father nods his head. "She doesn't even know me." Her voice is almost a whisper.

My father laughs. "She knows that you got hurt trying to save Chelsea. That's all she needs to know."

"Do you want a piece now?" I look at Willow and can see in her eyes that she wants a piece, but she is too afraid to say anything.

"I want one," Shirley says, and my father takes out paper plates and a knife from the bag.

"If it's okay with you, Willow"—my father looks at her—"I'd like to bring Quinn's mother by for a visit."

"Dad," I say, thinking it's going to be too much for her.

"She was here five days ago," Shirley says, and Willow looks over at her in shock. "We were all worried about you. You can have three bites," Shirley tells her. "And then maybe some more later."

My father hands her a piece that is so heavy she won't be able to hold it with her hand. "Water," she says, looking at Shirley. "Can I have some water?"

"Where is your cup?" Shirley asks. She looks at me and then the floor, seeing it all smashed. "I'll get another one."

"I have to get going," my father says and then waits for Willow to look at him. "Thank you, Willow, for today."

"You're welcome," she says and looks down at her hand. My father looks at me one last time, and I know he will be calling me later.

"Are you okay?" I ask her softly when it's just us in the room. "Willow," I call her name, and she looks up at me, and I see the tears filling her eyes. "I'm so sorry that you had to do that," I say, and her lower lip trembles.

"You don't hate me?" she asks, her voice as soft as a whisper. "After all that, you still think I'm a good person?"

"What are you talking about?" I ask, shocked at the words coming out of her mouth. "Did we not just hear the same story?"

"But ..." she starts. I hold up my hand, and she shakes her head. "But I enabled them."

"Enabled them," I repeat the word. "Is that what you did?" She looks at me. "I see someone who did what they did in order to survive. You, Willow Davis," I say her full name, her eyes on mine. "You are the epitome of a survivor."

Fourteen

WILLOW

"Enabled them," he repeats the words I just said. "Is that what you did?" I look at him as my heartbeats fill my ears. "I see someone who did what they did in order to survive. You, Willow Davis," he says my full name, and my stomach dips. "You are the epitome of a survivor."

The lump in my throat forms, and I want to say something, but I fear that if I open my mouth, nothing but a sob will rip through me. "My head hurts," I whisper, and he nods his head, walking out of the room to give me a chance to get myself together. My lower lip trembles, and then the sob I've been holding back escapes me. I put my hand over my mouth to cover it, but it's not fast enough because Quinn turns and runs right back in.

"Are you hurt?" he says, his voice filled with worry. "Shirley!" he yells for her as I shake my head back and forth.

"I'm ..." I start to say. He comes to the side of my bed, and he sits in the chair beside me. His face is filled with fear. "I'm ..."

"Just breathe," he says softly, taking my hand in his. His

84

thumb rubs over the back of my hand. "Just breathe." I close my eyes, trying to count to ten and get my heart to calm down. "You're okay." It's not my counting that gets my heart to go down. No, it's his voice. It's his voice, and his touch, and it scares the shit out of me.

I lick my lips and open my eyes, looking at him as he sits there in the chair with his shoulders slumped forward and his head hanging down. "How are you still here?" I ask him, and he looks up at me with his own tears in his eyes. "After hearing all of that, how are you still sitting here. Why?"

"How can you ask that?" He looks at me, his hand coming up to wipe the tear that has just escaped from my eyes. My heart speeds up for a whole different reason. "How do you not know that I'm not leaving your side?" His words hit me in the stomach as I think about the fact no one has ever said that to me in my life. I've been told many things. I've been made empty promises. But I've never ever had someone say something like that and feel it in my bones that he meant every single word he just said.

"What's going on?" Shirley walks into the room.

"Her head hurts," Quinn says for me.

"It's a low throb," I say, and she looks at me with her own tears in her eyes.

"You've had a long day," she says. "I'll get you something for the pain."

"No," I say, my voice coming out stronger than I want it to. "It's tolerable."

She tilts her head to the side. "Fine, but if it gets worse, you tell me."

"I will," I agree and close my eyes, not looking back over at Quinn.

I just told them a fraction of what I went through, baring my soul to each of them. I stared at each one of them, waiting to see how their eyes would shift, and they would look at me. But as each word poured out of me, and I showed them the hell that was my life, nothing in their eyes changed.

I hear voices, but the darkness sucks me in.

"She's staying with me." Quinn's voice plays in my head over and over again. "When she is discharged, she'll be staying with me." I turn around to find him, but all I see is the darkness.

"He didn't mean it." My mother's voice breaks into my head. "He wouldn't bring you home, not after he finds out what you did."

I run away from her voice, but then his voice comes in. "No one is ever going to want you."

I run in the dark forest until I see the light shining in. "You are everything." I hear Quinn, but the sound of Rosalie and Benjamin's wicked laughter overtakes his voice.

My eyes fly open, looking around the room, I see him standing at the window. His arm rests on his head as he looks out at the sunset. I wonder if he regrets what he said or if he's replaying everything I said. I watch him for a second longer until there is a knock on the door, and my head turns toward it at the same time as Quinn.

"Hey," Mayson says, stepping into the room. My eyes go from his to the black bag in his hand. My black backpack that I've had since I was seven years old. I don't have a chance to look at it too long before my eyes fly to the blonde walking in behind him.

Her eyes find mine, as her face fills with a huge smile at the same time as tears start to run down her face. "Is this a good time?" she says, not looking at anything but me.

"Um," I start to say and look down at my hand. "Sure."

"Hey," Quinn says, going to her and hugging her. "Are you supposed to be walking?"

"That's what I said," Mayson pipes in. "She refused to sit in the wheelchair I found at the front door."

"Would you two knock it off." She pushes Quinn away from her and then comes to me. "Hi," she says. "I'm Chelsea."

I'm expecting her to stand by my side, but she comes closer and leans in and hugs me as gently as she can. I hear her sniffle. "Thank you," she whispers. I don't have a chance to say anything because she lets go of me. Her eyes lock on to mine, and I see the love in them. She looks at me like I did something for her, when, in fact, I was the one who helped the person who hurt her. "I'm sorry," I say softly in a whisper. "I tried to get help."

"I know," she says softly and moves away from me and smiles again. "Are you okay?"

"Yes," I say to her and then look back when Mayson comes to my other side.

"I brought your bag," Mayson says, and my eyes light up. "This fell out of it," he says and holds out the locket that I kept in a secret compartment.

"It," I say, grabbing it in my hand. "It was my grandmother's." My voice trembles as I look down at the locket I got when I was seven. "She wore it every single day. The day of her accident." I close it in my fist. "She forgot to put it on." I wipe away the tear running down my face. "Thank you," I say, and he nods at me and puts the bag down on the bed.

"I need some help," Mayson says, looking at Quinn. "Can you come and help me?"

He looks at him and then looks at Chelsea. They share a look, and he nods. "I'll be right back." Quinn looks at me, and I nod at him.

My finger taps the bed beside me. "Willow," Chelsea says. "I don't know what happened to you."

"I told Mayson," I start to say, and she shakes her head.

87

"The only thing I know is that you got hurt because of me," she says and puts her hand in front of her mouth. She laughs and cries at the same time. "I said I was going to be strong for you." I look at her. "We are in debt to you."

"You don't have to," I say, not sure I can take what she has to say.

"You have to let us be there for you," she says. "Just give us a chance."

"What is in this?" Quinn says, saving me from having to say anything to her. I look over at him and see him carrying a big green bag.

"Well, that," Chelsea says. "Quinn's mom and I thought you might need a couple of things for when you get out of here."

I sit up as I look at the big green army bag. "We had to borrow Ethan's bag."

"I can't take that." I look at the bag that looks like it weighs a hundred pounds.

Chelsea puts her head back and laughs. "There are three more bags at Quinn's house."

I sit with my mouth open as I look at her and then back at Quinn. "My family can be a touch ..."

"They are the best," Mayson says, looking at me. "It can be overwhelming in the beginning, but if you just let the love in, it's going to be everything."

I can't say anything to either of them. "We should get going so you can get some rest," Chelsea says. "But if it's okay." She looks down nervously. "I can come back some time with my cousin Amelia."

"Um ..." I look at Quinn, who just smiles. "I guess so."

Chelsea claps her hands together. "She's going to be so happy," she says, and my head just turns around and around.

Chelsea walks up to Quinn and gives him a hug, and

Mayson shakes his hand. I watch them walk out of the room, holding hands, and then turn to look at him. "You have to take that bag." I point at the green bag. "And you have to tell them to take it back."

He puts his head back and laughs. I don't think I've ever heard him laugh so freely. "No chance."

"You have to." I shake my head.

"With the women in my family, you have to learn when to pick your battles." He looks at me, walking over to the pie and cutting a piece. "And this is a battle that one, I know I'm going to lose, and two"—he shrugs his shoulders—"I don't want to." He walks over to me, and I see his eyes crystal tonight as he smiles and hands me the plate. "Hopefully, you will be able to eat a bit more by tomorrow."

I look down at the pie in my hand. "Where is Shirley?" I ask him, and he looks back at me as he walks over to grab another piece of pie for himself.

"She clocked out two hours ago. Doris is here." He turns to look at me from head to toe. "Do you need anything? Are you in pain? Is it your head?"

"No, I'm fine. I was just wondering if I could have some juice," I say, then I look down. "It's fine. I'm good with water."

"I'll be right back," he says, walking out of the room, and I want to kick myself for even asking. I take a bite of the pie, and as soon as it hits my tongue, I close my eyes.

"This is the best thing I've ever tasted in my whole life," I say to myself, taking another bite, and then I look up when I hear footsteps coming closer and closer to my door.

Quinn walks into the room, and his hands are full. He walks over and dumps the juice on the bed. He picks them up and shows them to me. "Apple, orange, pineapple, grape, cranberry, strawberry kiwi." He holds that one up. "I don't think this is real juice, but who knows."

"Oh my God." I look down at them, trying not to let him see that I'm crying. How would I explain that I'm crying because this is the nicest thing someone has ever done for me?

"I also got grapefruit juice." He picks up the last one. "But I don't know if you can drink it. I have to ask Doris." He looks down at the bottle in his hand, and then he looks up at me. "Which one did you want?"

"You bought me all the juices, didn't you?" I ask him, surprised but somehow not. How do I tell him that every single time I turn around, he is blowing my mind with his kindness? How do I tell him that if it wasn't for him, I would still have some fear in me? How do I tell him that when I close my eyes, he is the one who helps fight off the demons?

"I didn't know which one was your favorite, and I was assuming you wouldn't tell me, so this"—he smirks—"was my last resort."

"Apple," I tell him, looking down at the bottle. For the first time in my whole life, I admit, "Apple is my favorite." He opens the apple juice, and he pours a bit in a cup and then holds the cup up for me. I take a sip as the sweetness hits my tongue right away.

"Little sips," he says when we hear a knock on the door.

I look up to see the most beautiful woman I've ever seen. Her blond hair is hanging down, and she smiles at Quinn. "I'm sorry. I should have called before just stopping by." She comes in, and I see how well put together she is. My head spins as I wonder who this person is.

"Mom," Quinn says, walking to her and hugging her. I just look at her looking up at him with such love, and my heart speeds up as I watch him smile at her. Then she looks back at me, her whole face filling with a smile. "Willow," he says my name. "I'd like for you to meet my mom, Olivia."

She comes to me, stopping by the bed, and her eyes fill

with tears. "It's so good to finally see you up," she says, and I look at her, confused. "I would come by when you were sleeping." She looks at Quinn. "We were all so worried about you," she says. She reaches out to grab my hand, and it's warm just like her son's.

"Um," I say, not sure what to say. "Thank you." I'm shocked that someone other than Quinn would be worried about me or my well-being. This is uncharted territory, and I have no idea what to do about it.

"I would have brought you something if I knew you would be awake," she says and looks back at Quinn. "I feel silly showing up empty-handed."

"You don't have to bring me anything," I tell her, hoping she doesn't feel bad. My hands shake but not from fear this time, it's from being nervous about making a good first impression. I don't know why I care. Everyone usually just looks at me like I'm dirt. But for reasons that I won't admit, I want her to look at me without disgust.

"I promise I'll bring stuff next time," she says. "How are you feeling?"

"Okay," I say and then look at Quinn. "He hounds me a lot." I hope that maybe if I tell his mother, she will make him leave. "I told him to leave."

"Oh, honey." She shakes her head. "Wild hogs couldn't keep this one away."

Quinn laughs and shakes his head. "Wild dogs, Mom," he says. "My mother is a city girl trying to pretend she's a country girl."

"You can take the girl out of Louboutins, but you can't take the Louboutins out of the girl." She shrugs. "I've been a country girl for a long time." She looks at me. "I miss the city sometimes." She looks at Quinn. "Okay, never. I never miss it." I just look at her. "I am so happy you are going to be okay," she says softly, squeezing my hand. "And when you get out of here, we'll take a drive to the city." I don't tell her anything else because there is nothing to say to that except I'm not going to be here for any of that. The minute I'm free to go, I'll be just a memory.

Fifteen

QUINN

I turn off the truck, grabbing the brown bag from the passenger seat, along with the bouquet of fresh flowers I picked up. The hot sun hits me as soon as I step out of my truck.

I walk down the concrete sidewalk to the front of the hospital. The flower pots on either side of the entrance are bright pink. Pushing the revolving door, I walk into the hospital. The cold air hits me right away. The smell of cleaning supplies will forever remind me of my time here.

Stepping inside, I press the button for the sixth floor. My foot taps with anticipation of seeing her. It's been ten days since she told us her side of the story. Ten days since she started to heal, both inside and outside. Ten days since I've seen her in a whole different way.

Three days ago, they convinced me to leave every single day for an hour while she does her testing or works on things with Shirley. So every day at three o'clock, I leave to go home where I take a quick shower and then head to my grandmother's house where she has food waiting for us. Everyone is itching to go meet her, but Chelsea told them it has to be done slowly.

The elevator dings, and I walk out, turning right. I see her right away as she walks down the hallway with Shirley by her side. Every day, she takes more and more steps. I watch her without her knowing and see that the bandage is off and her hair is tied on the top of her head. The circles around her eyes are slowly fading, and the bruises have all but healed.

"Hey there," I say when I get close enough, and I can see that her hair is a touch wet.

"Hi," she says, looking up at me and then back down. "We were seeing how many steps I can take without being tired."

"Did you shower?" I ask, knowing she did but then seeing that she is still wearing a hospital gown.

"I did." She smiles shyly.

"Okay, if you take five more steps," Shirley says, "you will pass yesterday by ten percent." I turn and walk with them back to her room. We walk at her pace, which is slow, but every day, she tries to outdo the day before. "And you did it," Shirley says when we get to her room. "I'll come back and check on you before I leave."

I wait for Willow to walk into her room, and she goes straight to her bed, slipping inside it. She puts her head back and closes her eyes. "Tired?"

"Just a bit," she says to me. For the past ten days, I've been trying to bring her out of her shell. I know it's not going to be easy, but one day, she won't be so guarded.

"I brought you flowers," I say, holding up the flowers to show her. "I thought it would brighten your day." I smile at her, and she stares at me, her mouth hanging open.

"What?" She leans in and closes her eyes as she smells the daisies.

"Why?" I bring the vase to her, and her eyes light up. "Those are beautiful."

I sit on the side of the bed, holding the vase in my hand and watching her smell the flowers. Her face looks angelic with the sun streaming in the windows. "Not as beautiful as you," I whisper, and I hold my breath with the flowers in the middle of us. I want to lean in and kiss her lips softly like I've been doing in my dreams. I fall asleep watching her and wanting to lie down beside her and take her into my arms.

"You didn't have to do this." She smells the flowers.

I get up, walking over to the brown bag. "I got dinner."

"You could have eaten at home," she says, "with your family."

I ignore the whole thing, knowing she asks me this every day. "Aren't you going to ask me what I have today?"

"Fine," she says, slipping her legs under the covers and closing her eyes.

"Do you want to nap?" I ask her, and she opens her eyes sleepily.

"No, no," she says, opening her eyes again. "I'm fine." She closes her eyes again, and this time, I don't say anything. I just watch her for a couple of minutes and then sit in the chair, taking in her smooth face.

Her eyes don't open again for an hour, and when she does, she moves her head side to side. "How long was I sleeping for?" she asks, trying to wake herself up.

"An hour," I say, smiling, and she nods at me. "What did you bring in the bag?"

I laugh at her and get up. "Well, Grams decided that you needed some more meat."

"She doesn't even know me," she says the same thing she told me yesterday, and I laugh at her.

"We have chicken fried steak with some roasted veggies." I take the container out and open it. "It's still warm," I say, putting it on the tray and bringing it to her. Her arm is still in a sling, so she has only one hand available.

"I don't think I've ever had chicken fried steak," she says, looking down at the food and then up again.

"Well, before you eat it, I'm going to tell you it's not chicken." I take the second container out and open it.

"What do you mean it's not chicken?" she asks, looking down into the container.

"I mean that it's steak," I say, sitting back in the chair beside her.

"So why don't they call it fried steak?" I look at her and laugh.

"It's because it's breaded and fried like a chicken cutlet," I answer her. "that is what my grandmother told me when I asked her."

She doesn't say anything else. She looks at me and then down at her container and then up again. "Do you need me to cut it?"

"I can probably do it myself. Or," she says, stabbing her fork in the meat and then picking it up, "I can eat it like this." She bites off a piece and chews it.

"Where there is a will, there is a way," I say, and she just shakes her head.

"Or when you're starving, you will eat it any way you can get it," she says, taking another bite of the steak. The burning in my stomach starts again when I think of her story. "Quinn," she says, and I look back at her. "Don't you have somewhere else you need to be?"

I look at her and almost snort. "Are you getting sick of me?"

"Yes," she answers. "But seriously." She puts down her fork. "Why are you still here?" She shakes her head when I'm about to say something. "I got it before when you were here to make sure I was safe. But I'm safe. I'm healing. I'm fine." She grabs the cup from beside her container. Apple juice that I poured her before I left because I knew she wouldn't ask

Shirley to get it for her. Apple juice, I know is her favorite even when she doesn't want to admit it. Apple juice that makes her smile just a fucking touch when she takes that first sip. "You don't have to stay here anymore."

"Are you done?" I ask, and she just stares at me. "Good, so maybe you should listen and listen good." I put my container down beside hers on the tray. "I'm here because I want to be here." My voice stays soft instead of rising like I want to. "I'm here because you are here, and I'm going to be here until you aren't here." I lean forward. "So you can stop asking me where I need to be or if there isn't someplace else I need to be, Willow. Because it's going to be the same answer every single time."

"But," she says softly, "I don't."

"You don't what, Willow?" I put my hands on the bed beside her leg, my hands in fists. "You don't want me here. You don't need me here." I look into her green eyes, and I'm sucked in, just like a whirlpool in the middle of the ocean. "It's about time you had someone here to make sure you're okay. Someone in your corner. Someone by your side."

"And you think that should be you?" She taps her finger on the bed, and I know she's nervous.

"I don't think it should be me," I say and then inch very close to her. "I know it should be. Eat your steak so you can have some blueberry crumble pie," I say. I see her eyes light up for just a second, and then she guards them again. "One of these days, Willow, that wall is going to come crashing down."

She swallows. "Or one of these days, you'll just not show up." She looks down at her food and picks up the fork again.

"Don't bet on it, Willow," I say and sit back down in my chair. My hands want to reach out and pull the elastic from her hair. Pushing it behind her ear and leaning down and kissing her lips that I've spent the past couple of days dreaming about.

97

She ends up eating four more bites of steak and a couple of potatoes. Her appetite is still small but it's growing every day. She never asks when the meal will be coming or tells me if she's hungry or not.

"You can go home and sleep," she says when the lights go dark in the room, and I look over at her. "And come back in the morning if you want."

"And miss getting a stiff neck in this cardboard chair?" I joke with her, and she shakes her head. "Good night, Willow."

She stares at me for as long as her eyes will let her. "Good night, Quinn," she says softly. She closes her eyes for a couple of minutes and then opens them again. "Thank you." I can see she is struggling with this, so all I can do is smile at her. She shuts her eyes as I watch her chest rise and fall as she succumbs to her slumber.

It's only when I know she is deep asleep do I pick up her hand and place it in mine. "You're welcome, Willow," I say and bend to kiss the top of it softly.

Putting my head back on the chair, I fall asleep. I wake when I hear her moan out, but when I open my eyes, I see she's still asleep. When her head goes side to side, I grab her hand in mine, and I talk softly to her. "I'm right here, Willow," I say, and she softly stops, falling back asleep.

When I open my eyes next, I look into the bed and see it empty. I jump out of the chair as I panic, looking around. I find her looking out the window. "I didn't want to wake you," she says, looking at me as my heart slows to beat normal seeing her there. "Where did you think I would go?"

I don't answer her because the answer scares me also. "I was just scared you fell off the bed," I say, walking to stand next to her looking out the window.

The black sky slowly turns a shade of gray, the yellow starting on the horizon. "What are you doing?" I look over at her.

"I'm watching the sunrise," she says. "Someone once said that it's therapeutic." She smiles slyly and turns back to look at the sky. "Almost like a restart."

"Is that so?" I say, smiling myself, and I put my hand around her shoulders. Her whole body stiffens, and she doesn't move. "That person must be really, really smart," I tease, and her body relaxes just a touch.

"Or he's a smart-ass," she says, and for the first time, we laugh together.

Sixteen

WILLOW

"How is your head?" the doctor asks, and I look at him.
"Fine," I say, and then he just looks at me. "No, seriously," I tell him. "I haven't had a headache in two days."

He smiles at me. "That is excellent news." He puts his hands in his pockets. "Which means this will be more good news." I look at him and then at Shirley, wondering what they are talking about. "I can discharge you," he says, and my happiness is there for one minute because then the fear creeps in.

"Are you sure?" I ask him, my heart pounding a mile a minute as I think of myself out of this room.

"We suggest you stay close to the hospital," he says, nodding at me, and I don't say anything to him. I can't form words right now.

"This is good news," Shirley says softly when he walks out of the room. "You are finally going to be free of here."

"Yeah." My mouth goes dry, and I ignore the stinging to my eyes. When I first woke up, all I wanted was to escape before anyone knew who I was. But the thought of being out there petrifies me, and I have no idea why.

"It'll be so good," she says, squeezing my hand.

"When?" I ask, trying to make a plan in my head. "When do you think I can go?"

"Go?" Quinn says, coming into the room. *Shit*, I think to myself. Looking at him makes the tears want to come faster and harder, so I avert my eyes quickly. "Where is she going?" I was hoping that all this might be happening when he was not here. He leaves every single day for one hour exactly, sometimes even less. No matter how many times I tell him to go or ask him why he's here, he has never left my side. No matter how many times I've sent him away, he's always here. No matter how many times I pretend to hate he is here, I sleep better knowing he is here. I know I shouldn't get used to it and that it isn't smart. I know that in the end I'm going to leave, and all he will be is a memory.

"As soon as the doctor signs off," Shirley says, "Willow is free to leave."

"What?" he says, taking his aviator sunglasses off his head. "Is that safe?" he asks, putting his hands on his hips. The worry is all over his face. A face I'm going to miss seeing every single day. I use the fact that he is looking at Shirley to wipe away the tear from the corner of my eye. I also take the time to get my wall back up.

"He said she can go but must stay close to the hospital," Shirley repeats what the doctor just said.

My finger taps beside my leg. "Is there a phone book anywhere?" I ask Shirley. "That you have around here." I ignore Quinn's eyes on me.

"Yes." She nods her head and walks out of the room.

"What else did the doctor say?" Quinn asks, and I look at him, my whole body filling with nerves.

"Nothing. That I can leave but have to stay close to the hospital." I still don't make eye contact with him because I don't trust myself not to shed any tears.

I can feel his eyes on me and all of the things he wants to say, but I can't pay attention right now. My mouth is dry, my finger can't stop tapping, and I think my body is going to start to shake any moment, and I can't show him this. I can't let anyone know how scared and petrified I am to leave here. I can't let him see how much I want to stay. I can't let him see that leaving him will be one of the hardest things I've ever had to do.

Shirley comes back in with a phone book in her hand. "It's been a couple of years, but I think it's still good."

I smile at her, trying to hide my nervousness. "Thank you so much."

I sit up in bed and open the book. "What are you looking for?" Shirley says. "Maybe I can help."

"Yes," I say, opening the book to the letter M. My eyes roam the yellow page as I move from one name to another. "How well do you know Mirth Motel?"

"What?" Quinn says in an almost whisper .

I look back into the book to make sure I saw the right name, my hands gripping the book so hard to make sure that no one can see my shaking hands "Mirth Motel." I try to make sure that my voice doesn't crack either.

"Oh, dear," Shirley says under her breath, and I look at her, confused.

"You aren't going to a motel." His voice comes out tight, and when I look at him, I see that he has his hands at his sides, balled into fists.

I swallow because there is no way I can afford a hotel. At this point, I don't even think I can spend more than two days in a motel. I'll let them think I'm staying there and then take off after one day.

I might be slower this time around with only one arm, but by tomorrow, this town will be a distant memory. I swallow down the lump that is the size of a baseball in my throat. "As long as there is a bed and a shower, anything will do," I mumble. I'm looking at the listing in the phone book, but the tears in my eyes make my sight blurry.

"You aren't going to a motel," he says again, and I can't look up. He turns and walks out of the room.

I hear Shirley snicker from beside me, and I look at her. "Honey," she says. "I give you credit for trying to be independent." She shakes her head. "But that man is never going to let you stay in a motel."

"My whole life," I say. "I've had someone tell me where I need to be. I can go where I want to go."

"I get that," she says, blinking away her own tears. "But your whole life, you've never had someone put your needs before theirs." A lone tear escapes. "It's too late to release you anyway," she says, looking at me. "I know it's hard. But try to see the good in it."

She turns to walk out of the room, and I look at the yellow pages, wondering if any of them take reservations. My hands start to sweat, and my eyes move on their own to look out into the hallway. Shirley stands beside Quinn, who runs his hands through his hair as she talks to him. I swallow the lump in my throat as I watch him for a second longer than I should. "He feels sorry for you." I hear my mother's voice and close my eyes, pushing it away.

"Shirley just said that you'll be able to leave tomorrow." Opening my eyes, I look at him. He stands there with his hands in his back pockets, and I take a mental picture of him. Even though I'm certain that if my eyes were blindfolded and they placed him in front of me, I could tell who he is just by touching him.

"That's the plan," I tell him, my eyes going back to the yellow pages. The book suddenly feels like it's a hundred pounds on my lap.

"Willow," he says my name, and I make the mistake of

looking up at him. He's the most handsome man I've ever seen, which makes him that much more dangerous.

"Quinn," I say his name and then look out the window at the lone bird flying in the sky. "Just drop it." I look back at him.

"I've learned in my family that you have to pick your battles," he says. "Some are harder to win than others." He laughs. "You'll see what I mean when you meet them." I want to scream at him to get out of my room. I want to scream at him that I don't want to meet them. I want to scream at him because I've never wanted anything more in my life, and I can't let myself wish for it.

"You did your duty," I tell him as I look at him. "You did everything you had to do. You found me, and you made sure I was safe." I swallow, trying to think about the words I'm about to say. "There is nothing left for you to do. This is the end of the road. I'm fine." My heart beats so loud it's surprising no one can hear it.

He just looks at me as we have a staredown in the middle of the room. He doesn't say a word to me. All he does is stare at me. And just like that, another chapter is closed. "I'm going to walk," I say, getting out of the bed and walking out of the room.

"Are you going for another walk?" Shirley asks, and I smile at her, hoping that Quinn hasn't followed me out.

"Just a short one," I say to her as I walk down the hallway. "Do you like living here, Shirley?" I ask, and she nods.

"I would never live anywhere else," she says as she walks beside me.

"Why?" I ask, and she looks over at me.

"We jumped from house to house," I tell her. "There was no place we went that I had a chance to settle."

"Oh, honey," she says with her soft eyes, and I have to admit I'm really going to miss her. "You need to plant some roots," she says. "Make a list of things you want out of your life."

"I can do that." I smile at her sideways and then look back down again.

I make a mental note in my head while we walk in the silence. Someplace where I feel like I'm home, I tell myself. Someplace where I never have to hide. Someplace where I can sit out on a porch and not have to worry that someone will tell me I have to leave.

"I have no doubt you'll see what is in front of your eyes this whole time," she says and gives me a hug. "I have faith."

I don't say anything else to her, and when I walk back into the room, Quinn is in the chair, his eyes on his phone as he types away. "Are you tired?"

"A little," I say, slipping into the bed, and no matter how much I fight it, my eyes give out, and I fall asleep. I wake a couple of times during the night, and every single time I look over at him, he is standing looking outside. *He'll be fine*, my inner voice tells me. Everything is going to be fine. I close my eyes again, but I don't fall back asleep for a long time.

I miss the morning sunrise, and when I open my eyes, he's in the same spot, but he has a coffee cup in his hand from the vending machine. "Morning," I say to him as I blink away the sleep. He turns around, and I can tell that he's been up all night.

"Hey," he says, turning. "You sleep good?"

"Better than you," I say, sitting up in the middle of the bed. "I woke a couple of times, and you were standing, watching out the window."

He's about to say something when we both hear a knock on the door. Our heads turn, and I see Chelsea standing there. "Good morning," she says as she walks in with another blonde behind her. "Did you just wake up?"

"I did," I say, looking at her and then the blonde, and I

suddenly remember she was the one who brought something to Quinn the other day.

"This is my cousin Amelia," she says, pointing at the girl beside her with her thumb. "Amelia, this is Willow."

"The famous Willow," she says with a smile, coming to me. "It's so good to meet you," she says, and I see that she is holding a black bag in both hands. "How are you feeling?"

"Good," I say, looking at her and the bag again.

"What are you guys doing here?" I ask and then look at Quinn, who hides his smile behind his coffee cup.

"We've come to take you home," Amelia says, holding up the bag in her hand.

"What?" I whisper.

"We've come to take you home," Chelsea says with a smile on her face. "Well, Quinn's home, but Amelia will be staying there so you can be more comfortable."

I open my mouth to say something but nothing comes out. "Um," I say nervously as I hear the sound of my breathing getting heavier and heavier. "I'm sorry," I say, shaking my head. "What?"

"They are here to take you home, Willow," Quinn finally says, leaving me stunned and speechless.

Seventeen

QUINN

"They are here to take you home, Willow," I say, and her face goes just a touch white.

She has no idea what to say or where to look. "Home?" She looks at me and then at Chelsea and Amelia. She's about to say something else when another knock comes from the doorway.

I look to see Shirley coming in dressed in her usual scrubs. Her hair is tied back with her glasses at the tip of her nose. "Good morning," Shirley says. Coming into the room, she sees Amelia and Chelsea. "Who do we have here?" Her eyes go to me and then to Willow, who looks around scared of what is going on.

"You remember Chelsea," I say, and I see her roll her eyes at me. "Ouch." I look at Chelsea. "You obviously were on her bad side."

"Shut up," Chelsea says to me. "Hi, Shirley."

"Hey, sugar," she says, looking at her. "How're you feeling?"

"Good," she says. "A little tired but it's fine."

"I'm Amelia," Amelia says. "We met once." Amelia extends her hand to her.

"Nice seeing you again," Shirley says, looking at her and then at Willow, who is just sitting on the bed watching all of this. "What's with the bag?" She points at the big bag they brought in. So much for being undercover or whatever it was that we texted.

"This is some stuff for Willow." Amelia smiles, looking at Willow, whose face is still confused.

"We've come to spring her," Chelsea says, bouncing up and down and clapping her hands with glee.

"Is that so?" Shirley says and then looks at Willow.

"I'm not going to lie," Chelsea says. "When I was finally discharged, I couldn't wait to get home." Her lips turn up in a smile. "Not that I didn't love you."

Shirley laughs at her. "How about we get you showered?" She looks at Willow, who nods her head.

She gets out of bed, slowly holding the bed to make sure her legs will hold her. She walks over to her black backpack and picks it up, then follows Shirley into the bathroom. "I'm fine." She looks back at Shirley. "I'll be okay."

"Do you want me to help untie your sling?" she asks, and Willow shakes her head.

"No," Willow says. "I did it yesterday by myself."

She nods at her and smiles. "Don't forget there is the button you can press if you need help."

"I won't," she says and turns around, closing the door.

No one says a word as we hear the click of the door close. I hold my breath, waiting to see if she locks the door. I am not the only one. Shirley does also. When we hear the sound of the shower, Shirley turns around and looks at me.

"Brought out the big guns." She folds her hands over her chest and looks at me from above her glasses that sit on her nose.

"I did what I had to do," I say. "She was going to go and

stay in a rat-infested motel." I shake my head. "I was not about to let that happen."

"You're a good guy, Quinn," she says. "If you hurt her ..."

"I'll cut him off at the knees," Chelsea says.

"I'll shoot him in the ass," Amelia says, folding her arms over her chest.

Shirley laughs and claps her hands in front of her. "Oh, she is going to fit in just fine," she says, walking out of the room.

"Okay," Amelia says, turning to look at me. "What the fuck just happened?"

"I don't know what you mean," I say, leaning back on the window. My legs are exhausted after standing all night, but nothing could have gotten me to sleep.

When I walked in and found out she was being released, I about jumped for joy. It was about time, and then the fear set in. What if she got a headache and her brain started to bleed again? What if she woke up in the middle of the night with pain and it took me too long to get to the hospital? What if I couldn't take care of her? What if she didn't let me take care of her? The pain was just too much to bear, and I had to sit in the chair.

My head was going around in circles, and I was trying to get my thoughts in order when she asked for a phone book and then mentioned staying in a motel. A rat-infested motel. A motel where she would be alone. There was no way in fuck I would let that happen, but she was fighting it all the way. So, I did what I had to do. I messaged Chelsea and Amelia and set a plan in motion. I stayed up all night playing it over in my head.

"That woman in there looked like the floor was going to open and swallow her," Amelia says, pointing at the bathroom door. The sound of the shower is still going. My eyes stay on the door as I wonder if she is going to be okay.

"She looked scared to death," Chelsea says in a whisper. "Did you not tell her?"

"Kind of," I start to say, and they both give me the death stare.

"Kind of?" Amelia says, and she folds her arms over her chest. "Kind of," she says between clenched teeth. "What does that mean exactly?"

"It means," I start to say, looking at them, and I know that the minute I lie, they will both smell it. "It means that I told her."

"And she told you fuck no," Amelia fills in the blank. "Idiot," she mumbles under her breath as she shakes her head.

I throw up my hands. "I mean, not in those words exactly." I look at them. "You don't know what I was going through."

"You are out of your mind, Quinn Barnes," Chelsea says, walking over to the chair and sitting down. "Forget about you, jackass." She puts her hand on her forehead. "Can you imagine what she is going through in there?"

"I can tell you what she isn't going to go through." I look at both of them. "She is not going to go through the fear of not knowing where she is going to sleep. She is not going to go through wondering if she can shower today or tomorrow. She is never going to miss another fucking meal in her life." I stare at them. "Unless she fucking wants to."

"Did you tell her all this?" Chelsea asks me. I open my mouth to say something, but then I close it when she tilts her head to the side, waiting for me to stick my foot in my mouth.

"What do you think?" I look at her, my hands getting clammy. "Do you think I could tell her all this, and she wouldn't fight me?" I look at both of them. "No matter how much I would have told her, she would have fought me." I don't add in that she always fights me with everything.

"Her whole life has been someone deciding things for her. Dictating where she lives, when she eats, if she showers,"

Chelsea says, wiping away a tear from her face. "And as much as I know that you are only doing this to help her."

"She needs to be able to decide for herself," Amelia says. "She needs to feel in control. For once in her life, she should be the one in control."

I run my hands through my hair. "What if she chooses to go to that motel? What if she decides that?" I look at them. "Then what?"

Amelia laughs at me. "Well, then you aren't doing a good enough job."

"I agree with Amelia," Chelsea says.

"Shocking," I say, shaking my head. "You guys are always ganging up on me."

"No, we are just smarter than you," Chelsea says. "Now, when she gets out of that shower, you are going to ask her where she wants to go."

"And what if she says no?" I look at them both. "What if, after all this, she says no?"

"Then you ask her why," Amelia says. "You ask her why, and you give her reasons," she says, and I'm about to say something when she holds up her hand to stop me. "And because I said so isn't the answer to anything." I laugh. "I'm not kidding, Quinn."

"She's not kidding," Chelsea tells me, and we both stop talking when the door opens.

Willow walks out of the bathroom with her hair to the side. "Um," she says, and I see her in the hospital gown again. "I don't have shoes."

"I have some," Chelsea says, getting up and getting the bag that they brought in. "I didn't know if you wanted flip-flops or running shoes." She unzips the bag. "So I brought both." Taking out a pair of each. "If they are too small, we can trade."

"I'll take the flip-flops," Willow says. "That way, if they're too small or too big, it won't matter." She smiles shyly at Chelsea. "Thank you."

"Did you need help with your hair?" Amelia says, going to her, and she just looks at her. "I broke my arm last year because someone didn't watch where he was going."

"You broke your arm because you were too busy watching where Asher was going to look in front of you." I pipe in. "Too busy looking at ..."

"We get it." Amelia holds up her hand at me, then turns back to look at Willow, who is rolling her lips, trying not to laugh. "Do you need help?"

"Um, sure," she says softly, and I look at her.

I look at Chelsea, who motions with her eyes toward Willow. "Go on," she mouths to me.

"Um, Willow," I start to say, and my tongue gets heavy in my mouth when she looks at me. "Do you really want to stay at the motel?"

She looks at me. "Excuse me?"

"Do you want to stay at the motel that you asked about yesterday?" I ask her again, and the whole room is so quiet you can hear the tick of the clock in the room.

"Or," Chelsea says, "you can stay with us."

"You don't have to decide now," I say. "You can. Um ..." Why am I failing to find the words?

"How about we do your hair while Quinn thinks of ways to say he's sorry," Amelia tells Willow, who just looks down at the floor. She nods her head, turning to walk into the bathroom.

Once the door clicks behind them, Chelsea lets out a snort. "What the hell is wrong with you?"

I look down at my hands and wipe them on the front of my legs. "Oh my God." She claps her hands and then hits her leg. "You're nervous."

"I am not." I shake my head, denying it.

"The cool, calm, and collected Quinn Barnes is nervous." She laughs really loud.

"Would you shut up?" I hiss at her, looking at her and then the bathroom door.

"You are nervous and scared."

"Seriously, shut up," I hiss over at her, walk to the door, and then turn around when the door opens.

Amelia comes out, and I see she has tears in her eyes, and I take a step forward. "Don't you dare."

"What's wrong?" Chelsea says and gets up, and Amelia shakes her head.

"I need to get her a pair of jeans and a shirt," she says, going to the bag and grabbing jeans and a shirt. "All her clothes are ripped and ..." She puts her hand in front of her mouth to block the sob that is going to come out of her.

Chelsea rushes over to her. "I'll take it to her." She grabs the things out of Amelia's hand.

"Bring her two pairs of each," I say. "Give her choices," I say, and she walks back over and brings the whole bag with her.

I walk over to Amelia and put my arm around her as she looks at me. "She is not going to some fucking motel."

"I know," I say, rubbing her arm. I also know that if she thinks I'm going to take her, she will be disappointed once again, and this time, it's going to be me who hurts her, and the thought alone kills me.

Eighteen

WILLOW

The soft knock on the door makes me look up. My hair is in a French braid, thanks to Amelia, who came in, and in a matter of minutes, it was tied up, and it felt great. "Come in," I say softly, sitting on the toilet seat. Holding my elbow in my hand, I'm waiting to put the sling on.

The door opens, and Chelsea comes in slowly with the black bag in her hands. "Hi." She smiles at me, and I just look at her. She is so beautiful, and her eyes are so kind. She quickly closes the door behind her. "I brought you choices," she says, and I just look down at the black bag.

My own black bag sits by the door in a low heap since all I had in there were two pairs of jeans that were almost bare from wearing and two semi-clean shirts. There is only so much you can clean while living in a car. "Um," I start, "I have a couple of things in my bag, but with everything that happened ..."

She smiles at me. "I know," she says softly. "But the good news is I have some things here." She puts the big bag on the floor in front of me and unzips the bag, squatting down. "Now, what were you thinking?"

My mouth opens as she opens the bag and shows me all

the clothes inside it. I've never seen so many clothes in my whole life. I also have never owned more than five things at a time. "We didn't know if you would want to wear jeans or if you wanted to wear shorts."

I look down at my legs, seeing that the bruising is still there, fading slowly. "Jeans," I tell her. "Always jeans," I say, and she takes out a white pair and a blue pair.

"Do you want to wear blue or white?" she asks, and I just look down at the two in her hands.

"I've never had white jeans," I say, and I want to kick myself. I should just take the blue jeans and a T-shirt and thank her.

"Then white jeans it is," she says, holding the pair out to me. "And how about a shirt?"

"Just a regular T-shirt is okay," I say, and she smiles and gives me a black one. "Thank you," I say, holding the T-shirt in my hand and touching the softness of it.

"Here you go," she says, handing me a white bra with matching panties.

"Um." I look down, and my legs shake with nervousness. "I don't know what to say."

"Can I speak freely?" Chelsea looks at me, and I just stare at her. "I don't want to step on any toes." She looks down and then up again. "I never want to disrespect you or insult you." She wipes away a tear with her thumb. "Quinn didn't handle any of this right," she says, and my finger taps the clothes on my lap. "He's a horse's ass for sure."

"We can agree on that one," I say softly. "I told him to leave," I admit, "every single day, but he never did."

"Oh, that is one battle you aren't going to win," she says, shaking her head and laughing.

"But," I start to say, and she holds up her hand.

"I know it's overwhelming for you," she says. "But this is

the only way we know how to thank you for everything you did."

I shake my head, the burning in my stomach coming up as the tears fight to get out. "I didn't do anything." I talk low, so no one can hear our conversation.

"I know you don't know us," she says. "And I know it's hard to wrap your head around, but you're family now."

"How?" I whisper.

"If it wasn't Quinn here sitting by your side, it would have been Mayson." She looks at me. "You both share a bond," she says, and she blinks away her tears. "I'm not going to talk to him, and eventually, he is going to come and sit with you."

"I don't know what to say," I say.

"Let us take you home." She reaches out and puts her hand on mine.

"I haven't had a home since I was seven." The words come out before I can stop and take them back. I regret them as soon as the words echo in my ears. I look down, not sure I can see pity in her eyes. I refuse to let anyone feel sorry for me. It is what it is, and what was dealt to me, and I'll be fine. "I'll get dressed," I say, and she nods her head at me and gets up.

"Do you need any help?" she asks, standing. I shake my head, and she smiles at me and walks out of the door, clicking it shut.

I let out a huge breath that I was holding in as well as the tears. I let the tears fall as I get up and slip the panties on, and I look down at myself. I've never had something so soft and pretty. I slip the bra on, putting my arm through the arm strap, trying not to move it too much, the pain getting less and less every day. Shirley showed me ways to do things when I'm changing so as not to move it.

I slip the jeans on and then button them before slipping on the black T-shirt. Then I tie the sling around me. I look at myself in the mirror, and anyone else would think I was just another girl. No one would tell that I lived in hell. No one would know that this is the nicest outfit I've ever had on. No one would know that I didn't even have a bra because all I could afford were bathing suit tops on the liquidation racks. No one would know that looking at me today.

I look over at the hospital gown that lies on the floor and bend down to pick it up and put it in my black bag, zipping it up and then turning to look at the other black bag that is bursting with clothes. I'm about to bend down and zip it up when there is a knock on the door.

I stand and open the door, seeing Amelia there. "Are you okay?" she asks softly, and I look around the room, seeing that it's just her and Chelsea. I look around to see if Quinn is inside the room. "He went to get the truck. I'll get the bag," she says, coming into the bathroom with me to grab the big bag. I bend, taking my backpack in my hand.

"You look so pretty," Shirley says, coming into the room, pushing an empty wheelchair. "Not that you weren't pretty before, but"—she smiles—"this suits you."

"Thank you," I say, slipping the flip-flops on and avoiding looking at her. I don't know how I'm going to do it without her.

"You ready to blow this popsicle stand?" Chelsea says, and I just look at Shirley.

"I can walk," I say.

"It's hospital policy, I'm afraid," she says, so I walk over to the wheelchair and sit down in it.

"We'll wait for you outside," Amelia says, looking at Chelsea, who just smiles and nods at me.

"Are you ready?" Shirley asks, and I look up at her.

"I've never been more scared in my whole life," I say, my hand shaking on top of my legs. "I've been in my share of situations in my life," I start to say, and my voice cracks. "But I've never been in this one."

"Oh, honey," she says, sitting on the bed next to the wheelchair.

"Hatred, I can handle. Hateful words just roll off my back. But this?" I point at the door where Amelia and Chelsea just walked out of. "That, I don't know what to do with that."

"You embrace it," she says softly. "The universe has turned now," she says, sniffling. "And it is time for you to see all the good there is out there in the world." The lump in my throat is so big I don't even think I can swallow. "You, my beautiful girl, are going to soar."

"I'm going to," I start to say and stop talking, not sure I should tell her.

"I'm going to miss you." She finishes for me, and I nod at her, and the tears come. She gets up and comes to me, hugging me. "I'll come and visit you, and you have to come back here in three days anyway."

"What if"—I wipe my face with the back of my hand—"I need you?"

"Then you call me," she says. "Quinn has all my information."

"What?" I ask her, confused.

"He asked me for my phone number right before he left," she says and smiles. "He might be a jackass, but we agree on something."

"Yeah," I say when she gets up and turns the wheelchair around. "What's that?"

"You," she says, beaming.

The black bag sits on my lap as she pushes me down the same hall she did when taking me for X-rays. The nerves are still there, but a different fear fills me. She pushes me into the elevator, and we descend to the lobby.

The hustle and bustle of people are all around us as she pushes me across the shiny cream-colored floor. People call out to her and say hello as we approach the big glass doors. She presses a button, and the two glass doors open, and the heat hits me right away.

I tilt my head, looking up at the sun, and the heat goes right through me. "Hey." I hear his voice, and I have to put my hand over my eyes to open them without seeing stars. "I was wondering what was taking you so long."

"Just saying goodbye," Shirley says. I get up and his arm wraps around me to make sure I don't fall.

He stands over me, blocking the sun, so I open my eyes. "You text me and tell me how she is doing," Shirley says to Quinn, who just nods as he helps me get into the red truck.

It smells brand new, and I look down to see that the leather seats shine in the sun. The dashboard doesn't have a speck of dust on it. "I will," he says, and I look over to see Shirley standing there waving at me as Quinn closes the door.

The black bag sits on my lap as the door opens again, with Quinn laughing. "I forgot to buckle you in," he says, and suddenly, he's all over me. His face is right in front of me as he leans his body over me to fasten the seat belt. His woodsy smell makes me close my eyes. "Are you okay?" he asks softly, and when I open my eyes, he is right in front of my face. I don't say anything to him. Instead, I just nod.

He smiles, and when he closes the door again, I let go of the breath I'm holding. I watch him walk around the front of the truck and get in, then he starts the truck while putting on his seat belt. "Are you hungry?" he asks.

"Not really," I say. My nerves have stopped me from even thinking about food.

He pulls away from the hospital, and I take the time to look out the window. I look at all the trees, wondering if I would recognize anything, but the trees all look the same as we drive toward wherever he is taking me. I make notes in my head of how many times he's turned, and then when we get to the town, I make a note of the diner. Then we turn into what looks like an opening of trees.

The trees cover the sun for a second, and then it's like the doors have opened, and we are on a road with a white fence on both sides. The green grass is pristine looking as it curves to an opening, to one of the prettiest houses I've ever seen in my life.

The white house with a black roof shines under the sun. Wooden columns line the covered patio that wraps around the front of the house. Two Adirondack chairs sit at one end, while a wooden swing at the other end slowly sways in the wind. "Where are we?" I turn to look at him and then back at the house.

"My house," he says, getting out of the truck before I can say a word.

Nineteen

QUINN

"This is my house," I say, and she turns and looks back at the house. I get out of the truck and walk over to her side, opening the passenger door. "Do you need me to help you out?" I ask, and she shakes her head.

She looks even more beautiful outside with the sun on her face than she has before. She struggles to get out of the truck, the black bag in her hand the whole time. "Welcome to my home," I say, stepping back once I know she is going to be okay.

"Is this really your house?" she asks, and I nod.

"It was my parents' first house," I say. "Then I made it mine. Let me show you inside." I put my hand on her lower back as she walks up the gravel driveway.

"But ..." she says, looking up at the house and then back to me. "But ..."

I walk with her slowly up the two steps toward the thick brown doors. Her eyes go to the swing. "There is another swing in the back," I say when I get to the door. "I added it when I moved in. It's my favorite spot to sit out at night." I smile at her, unlocking the door. "Welcome," I say. My heart beats so fast in my chest that I almost stutter the last sentence. I hold out my hand for her to step in. She takes two steps in and stops, her eyes roaming the whole entryway. There is a wooden table against the wall with a vase full of fresh flowers. "My mother said you couldn't come home without having flowers." I step in next to her and close the door, just in case she decides to make a run for it. Which, at this point, would not surprise me in the least.

"Your mother?" She turns and looks at me.

"I held them off as much as I could, but now that you're home," I say, putting my hand on her lower back again. "I can't promise that they won't drop by."

We take five more steps into the house and come up to a small hallway on my left. "Right down here." I point and lead her down to the closed door at the end. "This is the spare bedroom." I open it, and I have never been more scared or nervous to show my house. I also have never had a woman come into my house before. This is my oasis, and I've always kept it private. "This is where you'll be staying."

I open the door, and the sunshine shines right into the room. She steps in, and her feet sink into the plush beige carpet that my mother chose. "I can't take any credit for this room."

"This is ..." she says, the bag in her hand being held so tight that her knuckles are turning white. "I don't think ..."

The king-size bed in the middle of the room has a white and lilac comforter and a gray knitted blanket on top of it. I point at the wall where the bed is pressed up against. "That wall is the wood from my very first barn," I tell her, then point at the bench in front of the bed with the big beige cushions. "And that bench is the wood used in my grandfather's barn."

"You made it?" she asks, looking at me.

"I sanded it and painted it, but my mother did the rest," I say, walking to the door at the end of the other wall. "This is your bathroom," I say, and she follows me, her eyes taking everything in. "It's not big." I look at the white bathroom. "That is the tub my father had put in there when he built this house," I say, and she looks at me. "Built it with his own two hands. I can't even imagine changing anything. So my mother comes in every couple of years and decorates it. Hence the basket of towels." I point at the wicker basket she put in there.

"It's beautiful," she says softly, and then she walks back out toward the door. "But I don't know if I can stay here."

"Let me show you the rest of the house, and then you can decide," I say, and she just follows me. I want to tell her to leave the bag in the bedroom, but I don't want to push her. We walk back out to the hallway, and she looks at the stairs leading to the second floor. "There are a couple of bedrooms upstairs and a movie room," I say, and she stops before we enter the massive family room, where I have writing on the pillars leading into the room.

The most important work you will ever do will be within the walls of your own home.

"This is where I spend most of my time." I smile at her, walking into the room. The massive off-white L-shaped couch faces the fireplace with a television on top. "This is where I usually fall asleep." I point at one side of the couch, where a pillow and a folded blanket sits. "This is my second favorite place," I say, walking into the kitchen. "I redid it all when I moved in. My mother had it all in white, and I hated it."

She looks around, gazing out the bay window into the backyard at the pool I put in last year. She walks past the island and goes straight to the windows. "Is that all yours?" She points all the way to the back of the fence way in the distance.

"It is," I say, and I don't tell her that the land all around it is also mine.

"Do you want anything to drink?" I ask her, walking over

to the fridge and pulling it open. Her head turns to watch everything I'm doing. "There is sweet tea or lemonade."

"Quinn." I turn and look at her. She is wearing white jeans that are just a touch too big for her, but if my family has anything to do with it, she'll be filling them out in no time. "I can't stay here."

I close the fridge and walk over to the island. Putting my hands down on it, I try to rein in the anger I feel when I think about her leaving. "And why not?" I ask her.

"I can't stay in this house alone with you," she says, and my heart sinks. Her words slice through my heart.

"Do you not trust me?" I ask. "I would never ever hurt you." The thought that she would think I would hurt her is just too much to bear. I shake my head and look at her, walking to her. Standing in front of her, I reach my hand up to push her hair away from her face. "I would never ever hurt you," I whisper, my fingers touching the side of her face ever so lightly.

"I know," she says softly. "It's just ..."

She doesn't have a chance to say anything when we hear the front door open, and I see the fear creep over her. She steps forward, and her eyes go to the back door.

"Hello!" we hear Amelia shout out.

I take a step away from her as my heart hammers in my chest, my fingers still feeling her. "In here," I say, hearing her walking close to the family room.

"Hi," she says, smiling. "I put my bag in the first bedroom." She walks in and goes straight to the fridge and opens it. She looks over her shoulder at us. "You can tell your mother was here."

"Don't listen to her," I lean forward and whisper.

"Don't listen to him. He hasn't had a fridge this full since I don't know when. He usually doesn't even eat here."

"Oh, come on." I cross my arms and roll my eyes. "I cook my own breakfast."

"When?" Amelia turns and looks at me.

"I don't remember," I say, and then I hear her laugh. It's more of a giggle, but it's better than anything I've ever heard in my life. I turn and see her with her hand holding the bag pressed against her stomach. "I can cook."

"I'm sure you can," she says between laughing.

"Did you show her all the stuff you bought her?" Amelia asks, and I can see the look in her eyes change in the blink of an eye and if I wasn't looking right at her you would never know.

"I didn't have a chance yet," I say.

"Oh, good," Amelia says. "This is my favorite part of all of this." She claps her hands. "Come on," she says to Willow.

"You need to lie down," I say. "And I need to go and get your meds."

"Um," she says. "I don't have any money on me, and I don't even know where my bank card is," she says, and I see her squeezing the bag in her hand harder and harder. "I'll go get them tomorrow."

"Let's get you in bed," Amelia says, and Willow walks to her. "I can't wait to see it all," she says, and they walk out of the room. Amelia looks over at me and nods her head, and I know she will take care of her.

I walk out of the house, closing the door softly behind me and getting back into my truck. I pull out of the driveway with my heart in my stomach. I take one last look at the house before I take off, and I swear I feel her eyes on me.

Twenty

WILLOW

I watch him drive away from the house and then step away from the window. "I know it can be overwhelming," Amelia says, closing the walk-in closet she just opened to show me. "And I know you need your rest."

She walks over to sit on the bench at the foot of the bed, crossing her legs under her. My eyes take in the room, and I'm in awe. I have never seen a nicer room in my life. I have never seen a nicer home in my life. This is a fairy-tale castle where the princess lives. It's just another reason I shouldn't be here. "When you get up, we can put away the rest of your clothes."

I hold the black bag in my hand like a security blanket. "I really don't know what to say." I look around. "About anything."

"The good news is that you don't need to really say anything." She smiles and gets up. "I'm going to go and get some work done while you nap."

She smiles at me and walks out of the door, closing it gently behind her. I finally drop the bag beside my feet and walk back to the bed, making the mistake of sitting on it. I sink into it like it's a cloud in the sky. "I have to get out of here," I say to myself, kicking off the flip-flops so I don't get the cover dirty. I lay my head down on the pillow and make the mistake of turning on my side. Before I know it, I'm sinking into the darkness.

I feel a warmth all around me and then feel something put over me. I want to open my eyes, but the bed pulls me right back into slumber. When I finally open my eyes, I see that the room is almost dark, and it takes me a second to blink away the sleepiness. I look over and see the door open just a bit with a soft yellow light coming from the hallway. I sit up, and the blanket falls off me. Someone had put a blanket on me while I was sleeping.

I fold it back and get out of bed, going to the bathroom. The button on the pants take me a lot more time than just the hospital gown. I wonder if I should leave the room. I look out the window and see that Quinn's truck is there, but Amelia's truck is gone.

Inhaling deeply, I open the door and step out into the hallway to see if I hear any noise. The sounds of low talking have me stopping in my tracks. I take a couple more steps and look around the corner into the dimly lit room. I walk with my hand touching the wall as I look over my shoulder at the front door. The need to escape is becoming bigger and bigger. I stop in front of the writing that is on the wall.

The most important work you will ever do will be within the walls of your own home.

"You're up," I hear Quinn say and turn to look at him getting up from the couch. Gone are his jeans and T-shirt and in its place are shorts and a T-shirt. "I came to check on you, but you were out."

"I'm sorry," I say. "I didn't hear you." I look at the television and see that he was watching something. "I ..." I start to say, getting nervous.

"Are you hungry?" he asks, and I want to say no, but my

stomach has other plans as it rumbles. He laughs, and I look at him and see that his eyes look sleepy.

"Were you sleeping?" I ask, and he stops in front of me.

"I might have dozed off a bit," he says, running his hands through his hair. "That couch is way more comfortable than that hospital chair."

I swallow and look around when he walks away from me, heading to the fridge. "You don't have to cook," I say. "I can wait until tomorrow."

"You barely ate breakfast, and you skipped lunch," he says, taking a glass baking dish out of the fridge and walking over to the oven.

"I'll be fine if I have water," I say, and he slams the oven door shut.

"My grandmother made a chicken potpie, and it will be done in about thirty-five minutes," he tells me, his voice tight. "Did you want a glass of water?"

"Yes, please," I say, tapping my finger on my leg as he walks over to the fridge and opens it.

"Would you like lemonade instead?" he asks. I don't want to tell him that I've never had lemonade. I want to tell him that I'm not sure I would like it.

"I don't think I've ever tried lemonade," I say softly, and he turns to get a glass. He pours halfway and then comes to me.

"Try it," he says, handing me the glass. "I'm not a fan, but you never know."

He hands me the glass with the light yellow drink. My hand comes up to grab the glass, and our fingers graze each other. The heat goes right up my arm as I move my hand away from his and put the glass to my lips to take a sip. The tanginess hits my tongue right away. "It's good," I say, looking at it, "but do you think I can just have water?"

He laughs, grabbing the glass. "It's the bitterness that I hate." He walks over to the fridge and grabs a water bottle out of it, then returns to me and hands me the bottle. "Do you want to go sit outside while we wait?"

I try to hide the smile that spreads across my face by looking down, but his finger reaches out and lifts my chin. "Don't hide that smile," he says softly, his finger remaining under my chin. "When you smile. I mean, really smile," he says, "your eyes light up to a green that looks almost a crystal blue."

I look at him, not sure what to say. "I never noticed." I speak the truth, but I leave out that it's because I've never had a reason to smile.

"Let's go out." His hand slips from my chin, and he grasps my hand, pulling me out the door toward the backyard. I have to stop walking when I look at his oasis. The in-ground pool looks as big as an Olympic pool.

He turns to his right, walking next to the house on his covered patio until he comes to the swing. The same swing is in the front and made me want to run to it and sit down when I saw it.

Little strung-up tea lights are wrapped around the pillars that hold up the roof. "It's so pretty," I say in awe of the twinkling lights.

"This," he says, sitting down on the swing, "is what I added to the house once I moved in."

"Did you build it all?" I ask him as I sit down next to him on the white swing. He gently pushes it back and forth with his foot. Our legs touch each other, and I have this sudden urge to hold his hand. Just as he did in the hospital to calm me down.

"I did." He smiles. "I mean, my cousin Reed helped me out, and my dad came by a couple of times." He looks down. "But I wanted to do it by myself. I wanted to be the one who built it."

"Well," I say, looking around at the potted plants and then

the small two-seat couch on the other side, "it's the prettiest thing I've ever seen." I smile at him and then sit back as I take in the view.

The trees at the far end are so dense that you can't even see inside the forest, and the sound of a stream fills the air. "It's so peaceful." I look around.

"It is," he says. "I'll come out here and lie down after dinner." I wonder how many women have sat exactly where I am now, thinking this would be their house. That he would be their man.

"Where is Amelia?" I ask, looking at him.

"She's at the bar," he says, and I just look at him. "That's her second job."

"She has two jobs?" I ask, shocked.

"She does. She takes care of my barn during the day, and then she picks up shifts at the bar my aunt owns in town," he says. "She isn't happy if she isn't working. She always has to be doing something, and sitting around just irritates her."

I don't ask him any more questions. Instead, I look out and bask in the sounds of the night. The chirping of crickets fills the air. "It's so quiet," I say. "Like if you close your eyes, you can hear everything."

His phone rings in his pocket, and he gets up. "Food is ready." He holds out his hand for me. I look at him and then the hand, wondering if I should take it or not. "I'm just helping you up," he says, and I reach out and grab his hand. As soon as I'm standing, I let his hand fall and shake off the feeling of his warmth.

We walk into the house, and my mouth waters at the aroma filling the room. "It smells so good," I say and almost bite my tongue.

"It should smell good." He walks into the kitchen and grabs two pot holders, opening the oven. "My grandmother made this fresh today," he says, taking the potpie out of the oven, and I can see the golden crust. "I picked it up when I got your pills," he says, and my eyes are on the pie the whole time.

He walks over to the cabinet and takes two plates out. Walking back over, he cuts two pieces and puts them on the plates. "Shit," he says, looking at me. "I forgot to make a salad."

I shake my head at his nervousness. "We don't need a salad," I say. "The pie will be enough."

He nods his head and walks over to the island, where he sets the two plates. I don't move from my spot, afraid to get in the way. "Come and sit," he says, and only then do I move to walk next to him. He pulls out a stool, and I just look at him, walking to the one beside him as he laughs. "I was holding out the chair for you," he says, and I look at him shocked.

"I'm sorry, I didn't know," I say. "Why would you do that?" I ask him, confused.

"It's a gentlemanly thing to do," he says, grabbing his fork and scooping a piece of the pie. I look down at the plate in front of me and not only is the pie golden but it's flaky also. My fork slides right into it, and I blow on it a couple of times before I place it in my mouth.

The buttery goodness just melts onto my tongue, and I try not to groan. "Is it good?" he asks, and I just nod. "She'll be happy to know."

I eat until my eyeballs are full, but when I look down, I see I've only eaten half of what he's given to me. "I don't think I've ever eaten this much food," I say, looking at him. He gets up to get another piece, and he smiles.

"That was my plate," he says, and I look down at the half-eaten plate.

"I'm going to finish it," I say, and he laughs. "I didn't know," I say, my heart hammering in my chest as I look down and my hand shakes.

"Hey," he says and then calls me by my name. "Willow." I look up at him, and I have to blink away the tears.

"I don't mean to waste the food," I start to say. "I'm really sorry, and I know this is your house."

"It's my fault," he says. "I should have switched the plates." He comes back without his plate and grabs the plate in front of me. "I'll just finish eating this." He grabs my plate and fork and finishes what is on my plate. "See, no waste."

"Thank you," I tell him and yawn. "I'm going to head to bed."

"Okay," he says. "If you need anything, yell." I think about telling him that I would like him to come with me to my room. That I wake up at night and look for him. That I miss his hand holding mine. I want to tell him all this, but instead, I just look at him.

"Good night, Quinn." I turn and walk away from him toward the bedroom. I climb into bed, telling myself I'll leave in the middle of the night. I lie down, looking at the light in the hallway as my eyes start to get heavier. I'm going to sleep a bit to gain my energy and then leave. It's what I need to do for both of us. In the darkness of the night, I'll slip out, and I'll be just a memory.

Twenty-One

QUINN

I watch her walk back to her bedroom with her head hanging down. The look on her face when she was telling me about wasting food was more than I could take. I wanted to take the whole pie and throw it in the trash to make her see that I didn't care. Nothing, and I mean nothing, could prepare me for that look. I put the pie away and sit on the couch, the whole time listening to see if she calls for me.

When Amelia gets home after midnight, she just waves and goes to her bedroom. I get up, turning off the light, and I walk to Willow's room. I poke my head in there and find her sleeping on her side in a fetal position, and she is still wearing the clothes that she came home in.

I walk into the room as quietly as I can so as not to wake her and grab the blanket, placing it on her. I did the same thing this afternoon, afraid she would get cold.

Making my way back to the couch, I grab my own blanket, and I fall asleep until the sound of my alarm wakes me. I open my eyes and look at it, seeing it's five fifteen. Going to my bedroom, I walk straight to the closet and slip on my blue jeans and a black T-shirt. I walk out and stop in my tracks when I see her standing in the middle of the room. She looks like she is going to bolt. "Hey," I whisper, and she turns around. "Did I wake you?"

"No," she says. "I was ..." She looks at me. "Where are you going?"

With a smile, I go over and grab my boots. "To the barn." I slip them on and then look at her. "You want to come?"

"To the barn?" she asks, her eyes going big.

"Yeah," I say. "You might not come back with white jeans, but we can always throw them in the wash." I walk to the closet at the front door and grab a pair of sneakers I bought for her. "Let me go get you a pair of socks." I hand her the sneakers and go back into her room. Her black bag sitting in the middle of the bed makes me stop. *Was she going to leave?* I wonder, going to grab a pair of socks and then head back out to her.

"Were you going to leave?" I ask. She looks at me, the color draining from her face. "You were going to leave?"

"I was," she admits. "I've taken enough of your generosity."

"Where were you going to go?" I ask, trying to remain calm.

"I didn't have anything planned, to be honest," she says, setting down the shoes.

"Well, you aren't allowed to leave town," I remind her. I don't bother telling her that Jacob called me yesterday to tell me that she has been cleared of all wrongdoing, and she is, in fact, free to leave.

"I wasn't going to leave town exactly," she admits, and I hold the socks out for her.

"Here." I hand her the socks and then turn to walk to the fridge. "Did you even think about how anyone would feel?"

She looks at me, and I know that I should slow down and

bring my voice down a bit. "Did you think about how I would feel coming in and seeing you gone? Or Amelia?"

"No." She avoids looking at me. "The only thing I thought about was not putting anything extra on your plate. You have a business to run," she huffs out. "And Amelia has two jobs, so the last thing she needs is to babysit me." She bends as she slips on the shoes.

"I didn't think of anyone but myself," she answers. Seeing the tears she must have wiped away when she bent down, I hate knowing I made her cry. But the thought of her out there without anyone knowing is just too much. "I didn't think about anyone else because, for the past fifteen years of my life, I've only had to worry about one person and one person only, myself." The burning in my stomach comes out of nowhere, along with the pain in my chest. "But for the first time, I was thinking about someone else." She doesn't give me a chance to say anything. "Which way do we go? From the front or the back."

"We should take the golf cart," I say and turn to walk toward a part of the house I didn't show her. "This is the way to the garage," I say when she walks slowly behind me.

I turn the light on and open the garage door. She gets into the cart, and I slip in behind her. "By the way." I look over at her. "The house is wired, so it would have alerted me had you opened the door."

"Well, then there goes my plan to escape quietly into the night," she says as she looks ahead.

We pull up to the barn, and I look over at her. "Welcome to Barnes Therapy." I get out and wait for her to get out. "You are seeing behind the scenes."

I walk over to one of the red doors and pull it open. I walk in a bit and turn on the lights. "This is all yours?" she says from beside me. Her eyes are wide as she looks around.

"This is one of them," I say, walking in. "First thing I do when I come in," I say, "is start the coffee for my team."

"How many team members do you have?" she asks softly.

"At this location, I have about ten," I say. "Do you want a tour?"

She tries to hide her smile, but it comes out anyway when she nods her head. "Follow me," I say, turning to go to the closed door. "This is the office." I open the door and walk in to where an L-shaped desk sits in the middle of the room. She steps in and turns to look at the pictures covering the wall. "That is every person who has attended my therapy classes. There is more in the other offices also."

"You helped all these people?" she whispers, her hand going to her mouth.

"Yeah," I say, putting my hands on my hips. "I guess I did."

"You don't see it." She turns to me. "But it all makes sense."

"What does?" I look at her confused.

"Why you couldn't just leave me there," she says, and I don't want to get into this with her. I know she isn't ready for what I have to say, and I know that she has to heal first.

"You ready to meet some of my girls?" I ask, and she just looks at me. "The girls." I walk out and look over my shoulder to see her coming out and following me. "Usually, there is more light in here," I say as she walks down the gray concrete. "But in the morning, I only turn on the lights that lead down the path.

"There are ten stalls in this one," I say, pointing down the hall where five stalls are located on each side. Each stall has a cast-iron gate with the names written on the top of each door. I walk past each one. "This is Prada, Misty, Ivy, Daisy, Sugar, Holly, Sierra, Poppy, Luna, and my newest girl," I say, pointing at the last stall, "Hope."

"What exactly do you do here?" she asks.

"There are really five different types of therapy that I work with," I say as I walk into one of the stalls, and she stays outside. "Horseback riding helps with posture and muscle tone as well as coordination." I talk to her about the different types of therapy, and she listens to every single word, walking from one stall to the next as the horses come to the door. "You can touch them if you want," I say.

"What type of therapy would you recommend for someone like me?" She turns to me. "Someone who was mentally and physically abused and left for dead," she says, and I stop breathing. "Someone who begged every single day to die so their suffering would stop." She doesn't look at me as she walks to the next stall, and her voice remains even. "Someone who went twelve days without eating because I refused to forge a bank paper to get my money early so they could spend it." I was wrong before. This right here is the hardest thing I will ever have to hear. "Someone who couldn't even tell her birth mother what her fears were because she would help him and make them come true." My whole body goes rigid. "Someone who couldn't admit when they were cold or hungry or thirsty because it would mean I would get none of those things. Someone who would have to shower in a gas station bathroom sink and not a nice bathroom either. I'm talking about the ones where people shoot up heroin and leave their needles behind. Someone who would sleep with toilet paper in her ears for fear that cockroaches would crawl inside them. Someone who is woken up in the middle of the night and told that we are going and the only thing you can pack is two pairs of jeans and a T-shirt, which is why I always have a bag packed. Someone who doesn't even know what lemonade tastes like because all she could get is water. Someone who can't even admit to this day that there are good people out there, especially when it's right in front of my face." She turns, and I see the tears streaming down her face. I just look at her, unable to answer because of the lump in my throat the size of a fucking soccer ball. "What type of therapy would you give that person?"

I stare at her when I say the next words, knowing maybe she isn't ready for it, but knowing that there is no better time. "Everything."

Twenty-Two

WILLOW

I didn't want to tell him any of what I just told him. I didn't want him to know what I went through. Even if he saw me beaten almost to death, he didn't need to know the other parts of it. He didn't need to know the hell I lived in. That was my burden to carry and mine alone.

But with him here in the barn, looking at all the people who he helped, I wondered. Was I broken to the point where I couldn't be fixed?

I didn't even try to hide the tears, not after everything I just told him. His expression wasn't that of pity, it was one of almost rage and sadness but not pity. I walk to the next stall to see the horse when his words stop me from taking another step.

"Everything." I look over at him. "You deserve everything," he says, his own tear running down his cheek. "There is no one who deserves it more." His voice trails off at the end.

I smile at him shyly and walk all the way to the end of the stall, stopping right in front of Hope. "Hi," I whisper to her as she turns her head and looks at me. Her eyes almost matching mine, she nuzzles my hand, and I smile at her. "Good morning to you, too," I say while her tail moves side to side.

"You can open the top of the gate," Quinn says. "On the side is a latch." He points at the silver latch. There are two latches, one for the top and one for the bottom.

"Will it scare her?" I ask, not wanting to bother her, and he just shakes his head. I look back at Hope, who looks at me through the gated door. She is sizing me up just as I size everyone up around me.

"Just talk to her," he tells me. "As long as she can sense that you're calm, she isn't going to go crazy on you."

I unlock the latch and then look at her. "I won't hurt you," I say softly. The same words I've wanted said to me at least once. "It's okay." I hold out my hand to her, and she takes a step forward but then goes back. "It's going to be sunny today," I say, not moving my hand as she moves her neck a bit closer. "You are such a pretty girl," I say, and she sniffles or grunts. I'm not sure which one because I've never met an actual horse. I take a tiny step forward to rub her neck. "I won't hurt you," I whisper. "I promise." She doesn't move, but she does let me rub her neck. "What's your story, Hope?" I ask. "What's your story, pretty girl?" I look into her eyes, and I can swear she understands everything I say to her.

"She was left for dead," Quinn says. "She couldn't breed, so her owner just dumped her off at an abandoned farm." I look back at the beautiful girl in front of me. Her tail moves side to side. "She was skin and bones when we found her. She had one foot infected from an untreated cut. She had a scar on the side I'm sure she got from when they used to ride her and probably whipped her to go faster or whipped her to breed. No one will ever know."

"Oh my God," I say, putting my hand to my heart. She comes forward, and her muzzle smells the arm in the sling. She bends her head and hits the hand with her forehead.

"She likes you," Quinn says.

"Really?" I say, happy that she likes me. "How can you tell?"

"She's making you touch her," he says, coming next to me. "She is very picky about who she lets touch her."

"Does she let you?" I ask, and he nods.

"Only because I feed her," he says. "Do you want to ride her?"

I look at him, and I try not to show how much I want to ride her, but the smile on my face speaks volumes. "I don't want to push her and make her do something she isn't comfortable doing," I say, and he smiles.

"We haven't gotten anyone to ride her," Quinn says, turning and walking into the closet at the end of the hallway.

"It's okay if you don't want me to ride you," I say, stepping closer to her and rubbing her neck. "I won't force you to do anything you don't want to do," I say, and her brown eyes meet mine. "Promise."

"Let's get the saddle on her," Quinn says, and I move aside as he steps into the stall and talks softly to her.

"You going to let Willow take a ride?" he asks, his voice calm and reassuring. "She isn't going to hurt you," he tells her. "And I'll be right there." He ties the bottom of the saddle under her belly.

"Will that hurt her?" I ask. He shakes his head, grabbing the reins and walking out of the stall with her. "Let's see if she is going to let you walk her out."

"What do I do?" I ask, and he smiles at me.

"Just walk out the door." He points at the open door at the end of the hall where we walked in from.

I hold the reins as I take a step forward, and she walks slowly beside me. Her eyes roam the room exactly as mine do when I walk into a new space. "Are you looking for a way out?" I whisper. "I do that, too," I say as we take steps forward. When we get out of the barn, she looks around.

"She's never done that," Quinn says, coming out of the barn with a black horse by his side. "She trusts you." He smiles at me.

"Or she knows I'm just as broken as she is," I say and then look at his horse. The horse looks almost purple in the light. "Is that your horse?"

"This is Lady," he tells me and touches her neck. "Let me help you get on the horse."

"Um," I say, looking at him when he walks up to me and puts his hand on my waist.

"You are going to put your foot in this." He points at the silver stirrup. "Then throw your other leg over."

"Okay," I say, concentrating on the way his hands feel on me instead of what he's saying. He picks me up without forcing himself. My foot goes into the stirrup, and I throw my other leg over. I sit on her, and she haws. "I'm sorry," I say, and she doesn't move.

"Be easy on her," Quinn tells Hope. "Don't hurt her."

"She won't hurt me," I defend her as I watch Quinn walk over to his horse, and he gets on her easily. His whole arm flexes even bigger than before, and I have to look away before I start gawking at him.

"Ready," he says, and I just nod.

"We are going to go on a secret trail," he says next to me as our horses walk side by side. I see Hope looking over at times and then turning her head to look forward.

He walks through the field into the trees, and when I look back, the trees slowly close around us. "So what are your plans?" he asks. "When you are free to leave here."

My heart speeds up when he asks me this. "I have no idea," I say the truth. "I have nothing left of the inheritance." I look down, seeing Hope's head go down also. "I have never been somewhere that I didn't want to leave." *Except now*, I hear the words in my head. I don't look over at him, and I also don't tell him that staying here with him is tempting. "I guess this is as fresh of a start as I will ever get." We ride side by side. His hands never move from in front of him.

"If you could pick a place, what would it look like?" he asks, and I can see from my peripheral view that he is looking over at me.

"It would be where no one knows me," I answer honestly. "It would be where people would think I'm just someone else."

I look over at him. "Would you ever leave here?"

He shakes his head. "Nope, not for all the money in the world." He returns his focus ahead of him.

"Why?" I ask him.

"Well, for one, my family is here," he starts. "Second, my business is here. And third, this is where I want my kids to grow up. Running through the fields chasing their cousins. Going from house to house like a revolving door. Having someone have your back the whole time. I want all that for my kids."

"I've never had that," I say, his words echoing in my ears. "The longest we stayed in one place was before Benjamin. It was for one whole year. I even made two friends." I smile, thinking back to the two girls who lived in the same building as me. "Rosalie even cooked dinner."

"What happened?" he asks, and I think about lying to him, but at this point, nothing he hears will have him think less of me.

"She had an affair with a married man," I start to say. "All was going well until the wife showed up at the door. It turns out, her father was like some big shot, and let's just say we left very quickly."

"That must have been hard," he says, his voice soft.

"It was, but it was what it was, and nothing I could have done would have changed it." I learned that real fast. "Where are we going?" I ask, and then I stop talking when we come to an opening in the forest, and I hear the sound of water trickling.

I look at the creek ahead of me and then see a large rock in the middle of the clearing. "This is part of my grandparents' land," he says, stopping and getting down off his horse. "My aunt Kallie used to come here with my uncle Jacob when they were younger." He walks over to me, holding out his hand. I look at him and then the horse.

"I'm going to fall," I say, not sure I can hold him with my one hand and then slide off.

"I won't let you fall," he says. "Trust me."

I look at his hand and then back in front of me. "I don't want to fall," I say.

I wait for him to use my fears against me. Wait for him to just yank me off the horse. But instead of all that, he says words that cut me to the core. "I promise you that as long as you're with me, I will never ever make you fall."

Twenty-Three

QUINN

"Good morning," I say, sticking my head into Amelia's office. "You're here early." I look at the clock on the wall and see that it's only after eight.

"I have to leave early today." She puts down the pen in her hand. Amelia is my officer manager, and I don't know what I would do without her, to be honest. She comes in and makes all the appointments and pays the bills each month and makes sure everyone has their paychecks. "I have to get to the bar this afternoon." She looks at me. "We have a couple of bands playing tonight, and they want to set up."

"You could have taken the day off," I say, and she leans back in her chair. She is working two jobs, and no one actually knows this but she is silently buying the bar from our aunt Savannah, who wanted to just give it to her, but being the stubborn woman who she is, she fought her. I even offered to loan her the money, but she didn't want to take it from me.

"Did you just get back?" she asks, and I nod, going to sit in the chair in front of her. "You like the morning rides?" She picks up the coffee and brings it to her lips, trying to hide the smirk.

For the past five days, we have come to the barn at five thirty and taken a ride. "You know me. I love to ride no matter what the time is."

"Where is Willow now?" She looks around, peeking over to the door and seeing it empty.

"She is mucking out Hope's stall," I say, shaking my head. After our first ride, she watched me for a couple of minutes and then walked over to grab a bucket and made sure the rest of the horses had water. I told her not to, but she didn't listen. Instead, she just did what she wanted to. I told her to stop, but the way she smiled when she talked to the horses was every-thing. So instead, I watched her and made sure she was okay. "Then she's going to make sure everyone has water and feed them." I lean back in the chair and stretch.

"She's going to leave," I admit to Amelia, and just the thought makes my stomach ill. It makes my body go tense, and my anger comes to the surface. I have tried to ignore it, and I have tried not to think about it, but every single time I do, it just makes me sick.

"She already has one foot out the door," Amelia says, sitting up and making sure it's just us. "She hasn't unpacked anything yet," she points out. "She sleeps in her clothes at night," she whispers. "She rotates between two pairs of jeans, washing one and then wearing the other."

"You don't think I know that," I say. "Every single night, I go into her room to make sure she's covered. She hasn't even gone under the covers yet," I say, and I lean forward. "I have no idea what to do."

"What do you mean?" Amelia asks.

"I mean that I don't know what I need to do for her to relax," I say, frustrated. "I don't know what else I can do to make her feel like she's at home." I run my hand through my hair.

"I finally got her to try on two pairs of jeans," she points out. "And she accepted my cowboy boots."

I shake my head. "I bought her a new pair. She put them on the floor in her room next to the black fucking bag," I say through clenched teeth.

"Did she talk to you about what she is going to do after all this?" Amelia asks, and I look down.

"She wants to go someplace where no one knows her," I say, and the pain in my chest is like a punch to the stomach.

"Why doesn't she want to stay here?" she asks.

"Maybe because we know who she was before," I say, not even sure if that is really the answer. "I have no idea."

"So why don't you show her," she says, picking up her coffee again. "Show her why she should stay here."

"By doing what?" I ask, my leg moving up and down, thinking that maybe if I can show her, she might think about it.

"Show her why this should be her home. Take her to the diner. Take her out and let people meet her and start fresh." She shakes her head. "God, how are you so stupid sometimes."

"I'm," I start to say. "I haven't been sleeping," I admit to her.

"Whatever you do, Quinn," Amelia says, putting her cup down and looking down at her hands, "don't play games with her."

"How could you say that to me?" I ask, almost insulted by what she just said. "I would never do anything to hurt her." I get up.

"I never said anything about hurting her," she says, opening the drawer and taking out the white envelope. "I said don't play games."

"Meaning?" I look at her.

"Meaning that if you aren't in this for the whole ride, get

147

off the horse," she says, and I roll my eyes at her. "This is what you asked me for."

I grab the envelope and look inside. "Thank you."

"Oh, don't thank me yet." She leans back and smiles. "You still have to give it to her." She shakes her head. "Good luck with that."

I turn, not willing to give her anything else. I walk out and look down the hallway and see one of the stalls open. I start walking when I hear her voice. "You look so good today." She talks to the horse, and I have to say she is a natural. She knows how to touch them, how to speak to them, and how to get them to trust her. There aren't many people who can do that so easily. "Now you have a lesson in twenty minutes," she says, brushing the horse. "And I just know that you are going to be the best one out there."

In the past week, I've seen her come alive when she talks to these horses. I've seen her guard lower just so they can trust her. "Hey," I say softly so as not to scare her or the horse.

She looks up, and unlike the first day when she came in wearing white jeans and running shoes, she wears blue jeans that sit low on her hips with a blue tank top. Her face has gotten so much color, and her hair is getting lighter from spending all the time out in the sun. "Hey," she says. "I did those three." She looks at me. "And I have to go back and talk to Hope."

"Is she okay?" I ask, and she looks down and then up again.

"I think I hurt her feelings when I just put her food in and left," she says. "Usually, I talk to her and brush her while she eats."

I want to tell her that she probably didn't notice, but I can see how much this bothers her. "Well," I say to her. "This is for you," I say, holding out the white envelope.

"What is that?" she asks. I don't answer her because she leans over and takes the white envelope from my hand. Our fingers graze each other, and my whole body wakes up. Every night, we sit outside and watch the sun go down. Neither of us says anything, but I wouldn't trade that time with her for all the money in the world. Her sitting there with me. Her eyes going so green, I get lost in them.

I watch her face as she opens the envelope and looks inside. "What is this?" she whispers, her hand shaking.

"That is your paycheck," I say. She looks up at me, and I can see she is going to argue with me.

"I can't take this from you," she says and holds the envelope back out for me.

"I'm not giving you that money," I tell her, crossing my arms over my chest. "You worked for that," I say. "All this week, you worked over forty hours."

"I did not," she says, shaking her head.

"You get here at five thirty, and you don't leave until four," I say.

"But ..." she says.

"You come in here and ride Hope," I say. "Then you clean and muck the stalls. You feed the horses, and for the past two days, you've been bringing each of them outside for exercise."

"But ..." she says again, and this time, I see a tear form in her eye. I walk to stand in front of her.

"But nothing, Willow," I say softly. My hand comes up to stop the tear from rolling down her face. "You earned that fair and square."

"I don't know what to say," she says, and for the first time, she doesn't walk away from my touch. My heart speeds up, and I'm surprised she can't see it trying to get out of my chest. I feel like I just won the fucking lottery.

"You don't have to say anything," I say, moving my thumb softly over her cheekbone.

"I do have to say something," she says. She looks at the envelope again, and my hand falls down to my side. "This is ..."

She shakes her head. "You have no idea what it means to me." I don't say anything because the only thing I want to say to her will probably push her away. "This is the first time I've ever gotten a check," she says, still looking down at the envelope. "The first time I've ever gotten paid for a job." Her voice trembles. "It's the first time I have money, and I don't have to hand it over. I don't have to pay a drug dealer. I don't have to pay rent or a hotel bill. I don't have to pay for gas so we can leave the Walmart parking lot." She smiles when she looks up now. "It's mine. All mine."

"It is all yours," I say. "We can go down to the bank, and you can open an account."

She nods her head. "I don't know if I can ever repay you," she says softly, and I tilt my head to the side. "For everything you've given me."

I smile at her. "I'm glad I'm the first one to give you that," I say, wanting to take her in my arms and kiss the top of her head. "I have to go and talk to Amelia," I say, and she nods.

Walking out, I stop when I get three feet away from her and let out a deep breath. Turning, I look at her as she stands in the middle of the stall looking at the envelope she's holding in her hand. "You've given me life," I say softly. "You've given me a life."

Twenty-Four

WILLOW

I stand in the middle of the stall with the white envelope in my hand containing the check of six hundred dollars in my hand. In my name. For work that I didn't even know I was doing.

The past week has been a dream come true for me. Waking up every morning, I'm eager to start the day and itching to get up and get to the barn where my joy waits for me. The nights have been smooth sailing with no nightmares. No dreams of darkness, but instead of green trees and my girl Hope.

It's not to say that I was free. Oh no, those fears are ingrained in me. Fear that it would be taken away from me in the middle of the night. Fear that I'll wake up and everyone will know the whole truth about me. Fear that when I look into Quinn's eyes, there won't be the light in it, but instead hatred. So, I kept my bag tucked away close to the bed. A bed that I slept in every single night but refused to get under the covers. Just like the closet full of clothes all waiting for me, yet I stick to two pairs of jeans. I wear one during the day and one at night to sleep in.

I walk out of the stall and look down the pathway seeing a

couple of people I've met this week. People who had no idea I was a broken woman. People who accepted me with a smile and a nod. People who come in every single morning and say good morning. None of them looking at me differently because of who I was or where I came from. To them, I am just Willow, the girl who mucks out the stalls for fun. Who talks to the horses and brings them water and food. To them, I'm just Willow, and I've never been just Willow.

I walk out of the stall and head over to Hope's stall. "Did you eat?" I ask, and I walk to her and hug her neck. "I love you, pretty girl," I say with tears in my eyes. Tears because that is the first time in my life that I said those words out loud. Tears because I know what it's like to love someone for the first time in my life. My heart hammers in my chest so hard that I think I'm going to have a panic attack. I start to pant out, and Hope must feel it because she moves her head and I look into her eyes. "Look at us," I say, laughing while I use the back of my hand to wipe away my tears. "Two broken souls finding love." I laugh at the irony of it.

"Hey," Amelia says, sticking her head into the stall. "Are you okay?"

"Yeah," I say softly. "Just a bit—"

"Overwhelmed." She finishes the sentence for me. "I get it."

I look at her and shake my head. "You are the most put-together person I have ever met," I say. She has uprooted her life to move into Quinn's house for me. She has two jobs, and I think she sleeps less than I do.

"It's smoke and mirrors," she says. "I'm burning the candle at both ends, as my grandmother says, and I'm feeling it starting to catch up to me."

"Can I help?" I ask, and she smiles at me.

"Not unless you can make more hours to the day," she

jokes, and if I could, I would make it happen for her. "You have a doctor's appointment today."

"Oh, shit," I say, putting my hand to my head. "I forgot."

"Quinn is waiting for you in the office," she says, and I nod at her.

"I'll be right there," I say, and she turns to walk away.

"Okay, I'm going to leave for a bit," I tell Hope. "Hopefully, they take this sling off today." I smile at her and walk out, clicking the doors closed.

Walking toward the office, I see Quinn sitting in the chair while he's on his phone. He looks up at me and smiles when he sees me, and my heart stops beating in my chest. It does that every single time he looks at me or talks to me. Or we sit on the swing at night after supper, and our hands are close to each other. "Are you ready?" he asks, and I just nod at him. "Call me if there is anything," he says to Amelia.

"Have fun," she says, taking another gulp from her cup of coffee. "Good luck." She turns back and returns to whatever paperwork she's doing. We walk over to the golf cart, and in a matter of minutes, we are back home.

"I have to shower quickly," I say, and he just nods at me.

"I'll do the same," he says. "We have time. Your appointment is not for another hour."

I walk toward the bedroom, not looking back at him. I take my shower in record time, my arm hurting less and less. I walk out and go toward the pair of clean jeans folded on the chair. I pick them up, and I'm about to put them on when I turn around and walk into the full closet. Grabbing one of the pair of jeans that I've been dying to try on—a light blue pair—I slip them on, wondering if it would be okay if I used these jeans also. I could pay for them if they say anything. I grab one of the white tank tops and slip it on. I slip on the white running shoes that I wore one day to the barn and got them just a touch dirty. I get up and look at myself in the mirror, and for the first time, I'm shocked.

My face is fuller than it's ever been. My cheeks have little freckles that look like they are coming out. My arms have a bronze color, and my eyes, my eyes have never been so clear. I look down, not sure I want to think what I'm thinking.

I walk out and see that Quinn is in the kitchen wearing dark blue jeans with a white T-shirt, and his hair is wet from the shower. His eyes are focused on his phone. "Are you ready?" I ask. He looks up, and his mouth hangs open.

"You ..." he says. "You look beautiful, Willow." I smile.

I want to tell him that it's the new jeans, but all the words leave my head. "Thank you," I say to him, and he gets up and walks to me, his hand going to my lower back like he always does. He opens the door for me and buckles my seat belt for me. "I can do it," I say, and he stops moving. His face is in front of mine, and when I look into his eyes, I can see the little flecks of blue.

"Soon, you won't need me for anything," he says, his voice soft, and I swallow down the fear that is creeping up again. He moves away from me, shutting the door. I look out the window the whole time we drive.

Shirley spots us walking right away, and she throws up her hands. "Oh my goodness," she says, walking toward us. "Who do we have here?" I laugh, seeing her, and she hugs me softly. "You look like a brand-new person." She looks at me and then at Quinn. "What have you been doing?"

"I've been resting," I say and look down.

"Not with that tan, you haven't." She laughs.

"I've been hanging around the barn," I say and then look at Quinn.

"She's been more than hanging out. She's been working with the horses."

Shirley's eyes go big. "Oh, my."

"I get them water and feed them," I say, shaking my head.

"She mucks their stalls and makes sure they get exercise," Quinn says, and when I look up at him this time, I see how proud he is.

"Well, I'll be," Shirley says. "Now let's see how that shoulder is healing."

Two hours later, I'm walking out of the hospital with no sling on. "Does it hurt?" Quinn says, looking over at me and stopping in the middle of the walkway. "I don't think this is a good idea."

I laugh. "You heard Shirley," I say. "I just have to be careful."

He shakes his head. "I don't think." I laugh, and he just looks at me.

"You have a great, great laugh," he says, and just the way his voice is causes my stomach to flip just a touch.

"I haven't had much to laugh about before," I say, and then he smiles.

"Well then, I think this calls for some celebration," he says. "Let's hit the diner."

"What?" I ask him, almost whispering.

"We are going to go to the diner and have dinner," he says, grabbing my hand and turning to walk toward the truck. I try to wrap my head around all of it, and when he opens the truck door for me, I stop in front of him.

"I don't know if that's a good idea," I say.

"It's just a diner. Besides, I want to show you the town," he says. I look at him, and I can feel him hiding something, but I just don't know it yet. "If at any time you don't feel comfortable, we can leave."

I look up at him and see the smirk on his face. "You think you're slick." I fold my arms over my chest, and I feel a pull, but it's normal after not using it in three weeks.

He laughs at me. "Do you want me to buckle you in, or

can you do it yourself?" I glare at him, getting into the truck and buckling my own seat belt. He closes the truck door, and when he gets in, I look over at him as he gets his glasses on. He is the most beautiful man I've ever met. But more importantly, he has the biggest heart.

He pulls into the parking lot, and he looks over at me. "You ready?" he asks, and I shake my head. "I'll be right there."

He gets out of the truck, and my hand is on the handle when he opens my door. He holds out his hand to help me, and I take it. I'm expecting him to drop my hand once my feet hit the pavement, but he doesn't.

I look around and see groups of teenagers all over the place. "What's going on?" I ask, and he looks at me.

"It's Friday night," he says. "All the kids meet here before they go and watch the Friday night game."

"That really happens?" I ask, and he smiles at me. "I thought it was just in the movies."

He shakes his head and is about to say something when someone calls his name. "Quinn." I look over and see someone who looks very much like Quinn come jogging to him.

"Hey," Quinn says, giving him a hug. "Are you behaving?"

"As much as you did at my age," the boy says. "Hey there, darlin'," he says to me. Quinn pushes his shoulder back, and he laughs.

"Back off, little brother," he says to him, and I can see it. They have the same eyes, but his hair is black instead of blond. "Willow, this is Reed."

"It's nice to meet you," I say, and he just smiles at me when someone calls his name.

"I have to go." He turns back to us. "I'll see you Sunday," he tells his brother. "And I hope to see you soon, darlin'."

"Remember that time you thought I shot you in the ass."

Quinn glares at him while Reed just laughs. "Keep that darlin' shit up, and I will."

He holds up his hands, laughing. "Duly noted," he says, walking backward.

"Did you just threaten to shoot your brother?" I look at him as we continue walking into the diner.

"If he called you darlin' one more time, I would consider it." He opens the door with his free hand and holds it open for me to step in. "My mother would whip my ass, but it would be worth it."

I shake my head as I step into the diner, wearing a smile on my face. I see the whole diner is full. Teenagers fill some of the booths and tables as the sound of laughter fills the room. I look around and keep my head down. I expect people to look at me and point. I expect people to watch my every move. I expect them to look down on me. But none of that happens. No one notices me. No one points. No one wrinkles their nose at me. No one treats me like I have a disease or shies away from me when we walk in.

"Are you okay?" Quinn says from beside me, and for the first time in my whole life, I feel like this is somewhere I could live. This could be home for me. I can picture myself living here and being one of them.

"I'm fine," I say to him, and fuck do I ever mean it.

Twenty-Five

QUINN

I hold her hand walking into the diner because if she is feeling anything, her body will go tight, and I'll feel it.

The last thing I want is for her not to be comfortable here. My goal is to show her why she should stay, and if she doesn't like it ... well, I wasn't even going to go there because there was no way I was going to let her leave.

"Where do you want to sit?" she asks. Someone bumps into her, and she stumbles into my arms. I wrap an arm around her waist to protect her from falling. Her hands go to my chest as she looks up with big eyes. "You okay?"

"I'm so sorry," one of the teenagers says as she turns to walk out.

"Do you want to go?" I ask, hoping she thinks about her answer so I can have her in my arms longer than I should.

"Hey, you two," I hear behind me and look to see Chelsea and Mayson. "Oh, you got the sling off," she says when she sees both of Willow's hands.

"I did," Willow says and takes a step out of my arms. The arm wrapped around her waist falls to my side.

"That's amazing," Chelsea says. "Let's grab that booth."

She points at a booth in the back that was just vacated by six teenagers.

Chelsea slips her hand in Mayson's as they walk to the booth. "If you want to go."

"I'm good," she says, smiling, and turns to follow Chelsea. Her head dips just a bit as she tries not to make eye contact with anyone.

She slips into the booth in front of Chelsea, and I slip in beside her in front of Mayson. I see her eyes roaming all over the place as she takes it all in. "Are those jukeboxes?" she asks, pointing at a couple who are still here in some of the booths.

"Yes," I tell her. "And they have songs from the eighties."

Her eyes light up, and her mouth opens. "That is pretty cool," she says, and then I hand her a menu. "I'm not hungry," she says, ignoring my eyes. "I'll have water."

My heart speeds up, and I'm not the only one. "You will not," Mayson says, looking at her, and then at Chelsea, who looks at him like he hangs the moon.

"I don't really want anything," Willow says, and I can see her finger tap the table, which means she's worried about something.

"The burgers are where it's at," Chelsea says, looking at her. "But it's a bit too much for me, so you want to split it?" I wait to see what she is going to say. Knowing full well it isn't too much for Chelsea because she always finishes her burger.

The waitress comes over, and I order a double burger for myself with fries and rings with two root beer floats. Chelsea looks at me and orders the same thing. Mayson orders two of whatever I ordered, and he looks at the table. "I haven't eaten all day."

Chelsea starts talking about her week at the new clinic where she's working, and when the root beer floats come, I put one in front of Willow, who just looks at me.

"What is this?" she asks, confused as to what the brown bubbly liquid is with the scoop of ice cream floating on top.

"This," I say, handing her the long spoon and a straw, "is a root beer with a scoop of ice cream."

"It's to die for," Chelsea says of her own now. "Try it."

She puts the straw in and takes a sip. "That is a little weird," she says and takes another sip, this time coughing. "The bubbles came out of my nose."

I shake my head and watch her work her way through it until the burgers arrive. I look at Mayson, who takes one of his burger trays and hands it to Willow. "Here, I'm not hungry anymore." I look at him, knowing he is lying, and then I look at Chelsea, who looks at me and then down, hiding a smile. "If you don't eat it, it's going to go to waste."

"Dig in," I say as she just looks down at the burger and then up again. "Eat." Her eyes just look at me, and I can tell that her head is spinning, so I lean in and whisper in her ear, "You can pay me back when you cash your check."

She tries to hide her smile as she looks down and grabs the burger in her hand and takes a bite. We eat in silence, and when I look over, she has polished the whole burger and almost all the fries. "Was it good?" I ask, and she nods her head at me and hides a smile.

I get up and hold my hand out for Willow, who slides out of the booth. "We didn't pay the bill," she says, looking around, and we all laugh.

"Oh, we never pay the bill," Chelsea says. "They put it on the tab, and our parents pay it."

"Wait?" Willow says. "What?"

"They started doing this when we were in high school, and even when we want to pay, they ignore us," Chelsea says, sliding out of the booth and taking Mayson's hand.

We walk out of the restaurant, and the sun is setting. "We

are going to head home," Chelsea says. "See you on Sunday." She hugs Willow, who just looks at me, and I know she has questions.

When we pull up to the house, I get out, and she is out of the truck by the time I walk around. "Do you want to watch the sun set?" I ask. She smiles and nods.

I slip my hand in hers as though it's a normal thing to do, and she lets me. Her small cold hand sits in my big warm one. We walk around the house as I close the gate behind us, the soft breeze blowing her hair. "It's not hot," she says as we walk up the step toward the swing.

I sit beside her as she looks off into the distance. "Did you have fun?" I ask her, putting my arm across the back of the swing.

"I did," she says. "And you were right. The burger was amazing." She looks down and then up. "What's on Sunday?"

"Every Sunday, my grandparents have a barbecue. It started before I was born, and it has just grown into this big thing. Practically the whole town shows up." My thumb rubs her shoulder softly, hoping she doesn't move away from me.

"But ..." She looks at me. "When I was in the hospital, you never left."

"Okay?" I don't know if she's asking me or telling me.

"You didn't go?" The wind picks up just a touch, and the hair flies in her face. My hand comes up to push the hair away from her face. "You never left me."

My thumb moves across her cheekbones. "No," I whisper, my head is moving closer to hers. "I never left your side." My head dips just a touch more, and I am so close to her lips I can taste the kiss.

"Quinn, I should get to bed." My hand falls from her face, and I just look at her.

"Let's get inside," I say, getting up and holding out my

hand to her. She slips her hand in mine, and even though I hate myself for not taking the kiss I've been dreaming about, I won't push her. She is the one who will lead where this goes. We are going to do things on her time.

I unlock the door, and she walks in before me. "Thank you," she says and then turns around. "For today." She wears the biggest smile I've seen on her face. "Even the root beer float."

I laugh. "Anytime, Willow," I say. She nods and heads to her bedroom. "Good night, Willow." She looks over her shoulder at me. "Sweet dreams."

"You, too, Quinn," she says softly. I walk to the couch and turn the television on, but my head is on the girl sleeping in the bedroom. I doze off and open my eyes when I hear Amelia come in. I look over and see that it's just after two in the morning. I wait for her to go to her room before I get up and walk to her bedroom.

I push open her door and see her sleeping in the middle of the room, wearing a pair of jeans and a T-shirt. Walking in, I see the two black bags side by side. Something eats me inside at seeing that. I put the cover over her and walk out before I unpack the bag for her. When I slide into bed, my eyes don't close all night. All I can do is see the two bags in my head. Every single time I close my eyes, that's all I see.

When the alarm rings the next day, I'm not surprised she's already waiting for me in the kitchen. "Morning," I say, almost grunting at her. My nerves are on edge when I see her wearing what she wore yesterday to the barn. "Ready?" I ask, and she nods and walks outside.

She gets into the golf cart beside me, and I can't help the anger that runs through me. I open the door and saddle the horses, then we ride side by side, neither of us saying anything. I don't trust myself to say anything to her.

When we get back two hours later, I get off the horse first, and then she slides off Hope. "Is everything okay?" she asks, holding Hope's reins as we walk back into the barn. "You're very quiet today."

"Yeah," I say and then turn to look at her.

"Are you okay?" she asks again, and I know I have to tread carefully. I know I shouldn't say even one word, but looking at her, with the sun shining on her and seeing her so much stronger, I can't stop the words from coming out.

"Why haven't you unpacked?" I ask, and she just looks at me. "You haven't unpacked. You sleep on the top of your bed. When ..." I ask, throwing my hands up. "When are you going to fucking unpack?"

"I don't ..." She looks down, and I shake my head. God, how can she not see how much I want her here?

"Yeah, I know you don't want to." I shake my head and walk into the barn. I have to get away from her before I say things that will hurt her even more.

I listen to her put Hope in her stall as I walk into the office and close the door. I sit down behind my desk, letting the anger leave me. I put my head back and close my eyes. I hear people arrive, and I walk out of the office. I start the coffee, and only when it's done and I've had a cup do I walk down to offer her a bottle of water. I poke my head into the stall and see that she isn't there. I check all the stalls, and I can't find her anywhere.

"Have you seen Willow?" I ask Asher, who is unloading bales of hay.

I look around and see that the golf cart is gone. "Fuck," I say and then look at him. "I need your truck." He must hear the panic in my voice because he closes the back of the truck as I run toward the driver's side. I get home and see that my truck is the only one in the driveway.

163

I put the truck in park and get out, jogging to the front door. "Willow!" I yell her name and run to her bedroom, seeing it empty. My eyes scan the room, and I see only one black bag there. "Fuck," I hiss, the pain in my heart coming on so strong I have to sit down on the bed. "She's gone."

Twenty-Six

WILLOW

"Thank you." I look over at Amelia sitting beside me. "For taking me."

She shakes her head and smiles at me. "Anything for you," she says softly, and my heart almost explodes in my chest. No one has ever said those words. Better yet, I've never believed them before last month.

After I left the barn, I took the golf cart to the house and walked into the house the same time that Amelia was stumbling to the coffee machine. She took one look at me and asked me what was wrong. I couldn't really say anything to her. I didn't trust myself not to sob. How could he think I don't want to unpack? How can he assume such a thing? "Can you take me to see Mayson?" I ask because if anyone in the whole town knows or has seen what I've seen, I know it's Mayson.

"I know you came home late this morning," I say, and she shrugs.

"I'll nap later," she says. "Besides, I'm hoping that Chelsea will whip me up some biscuits and gravy." She smiles so big as we turn into the driveway. I rub my sweaty palms on my jeans before reaching for the door handle to open the door. The sun shines so bright in the sky I have to squint to see the white door.

I walk for the front door, following Amelia, and she looks over at me. "Normally, I would just walk in, but when you come face-to-face with a naked ass even one time, you learn your lesson." I laugh at her as she rings the bell. "If only I was kidding."

The sound of the lock clicking open makes my heart speed up just a touch. Maybe this isn't the greatest idea I've had. I'm about to turn to Amelia and make a run for it when the door opens. "Oh, she rings." Chelsea stands there wearing shorts and a tank top. A coffee cup in her right hand comes up to her mouth as she tries to hide the smile that fills her face. But the crinkle by her eyes shows us that she is smiling.

"Oh, shut your pie hole," Amelia says, pushing into the house and then halting in her tracks. "Are we all decent?"

"He's in the shower," Chelsea says.

"Phew," Amelia says, walking into the house. "Did you cook yet?"

"I was just starting to," she says, closing the door behind me. "Did you just come for food?" she asks, looking at Amelia, then at me.

"Yes for me. No for Willow."

Chelsea looks over at me. "I was wondering if I could talk to Mayson." I look down. "It's fine if he doesn't want to, or if you don't want me to."

"Willow," she says my name softly. "He would love nothing more."

I just nod as she pulls my hand to bring me into the house. I take a second to look around. Pictures of the family hang along the walls, and my eyes stop on one with a woman and a man sitting in two chairs with everyone behind them. "That was last Christmas," Chelsea says. "Finally, everyone was in one place at the same time." I smile over at her as my eyes find Quinn's right away. He stands with his arm around his father.

"Can you make biscuits?" Amelia sticks her head around the corner. "And gravy."

Chelsea shakes her head and walks ahead, and I follow her, the open concept very much like Quinn's house. "Coffee?" Amelia says, starting the coffee. I'm about to tell her no. The last thing I need in me is coffee, not with my nerves.

"Hey." I hear Mayson behind me and see him coming out of what I'm assuming is the bedroom. His hair is still wet as he walks closer and kisses Chelsea on the lips and then looks at me. "Good to see you."

"I rang the bell," Amelia says, leaning on the counter with her coffee mug in her hand. Mayson chuckles and shakes his head. "There are things you can't erase from your mind."

"You didn't see shit," he tells her.

"I saw your ass, and then I saw that one"—she points at Chelsea—"running away from you."

"I was not running." Chelsea looks at Mayson.

"I had my weapon exposed," Mayson cuts in. "She was running for cover."

I roll my lips while Amelia puts a hand to her stomach. "I'm going to be sick."

"Why don't I start cooking, and you show Willow the backyard," Chelsea says, and Mayson looks over at me and nods his head.

"Right this way," he says, turning and walking out of the house. I follow him, my heart is beating so fast in my chest, and my mouth is suddenly so dry. I should have gotten a water bottle. He walks outside, and I see the difference now. There is no pool here, just a hammock. "Do you mind sitting on the steps?" He points at the concrete steps, and I shake my head. He walks first, and I follow his lead, sitting down next to him.

He must sense my nervousness because he talks first. "We come out here every morning to watch the sunrise."

I laugh, looking down at my hands. "This family is obsessed with sunrises and sunsets."

"I think if you grew up like them, you can see the beauty in it." His voice goes soft. "But if you grew up like us, it's just a sign you are going to live another day."

I look over at him. "I ..." The only word that comes out of my mouth. "I'm trying to see it."

"It took me a while," he admits.

"Are you okay talking about it?" I ask him. "I don't want to make you feel weird or uncomfortable."

"There is no one in this whole world besides me and you," he says, "who understand what the other is going through." Those words hit me right in the chest.

"I never thought I would ever meet someone who would know what I felt," I say softly, the tears coming even though I have been fighting them off. "I would lie awake at night."

"And look up, wondering what you did." I look over at him. "It took me a long time to figure out there wasn't anything I could have changed."

"How did you do it?" I ask. "How did you take that leap of faith?" He doesn't have a chance to say a word. "How did you take that chance?" I look down. "Like I want to. I want to do it all. Take the help that people give me." He nods his head, knowing that I need to talk this out. "I want to smile and be okay with smiling and not smile, looking over my shoulder to see if someone is watching. Because you know the minute they see you smiling, they have leverage over you."

"That was the hardest part for me, too," he says softly to me. "To see the good in people out there. To know they weren't taking notes to use on you later."

"Exactly," I say. "Quinn, he's ..."

"I know," he says, nodding his head. "But not everyone is

our parents. There are good people out there," he says. "People who would put their lives before others. If I didn't see it with my own eyes, I wouldn't believe it either."

"Quinn, he asked me why I haven't unpacked," I say.

"He's afraid," he says, and I just look at him with my mouth hanging open. How could the strongest man in the world be scared? "He's afraid you'll leave him. Afraid he'll wake up one day and you'll be gone."

I close my mouth and then open it again. "Yet the only thing you are afraid of is that they'll see the bad in you. That they will see everything that Benjamin did and put you with him."

"I am not like him or my birth mother," I say, my voice shaking now. "I would never be them."

"See." He points at me. "That right there is you taking your life back."

"I like it here," I say and then look down. "A lot."

"It's a great place to settle down," he says. "I knew that after I came to visit Ethan. I knew I wanted to live in a town where everyone knew me, but not as Braxton but as Mayson. If there is anywhere to do that, it's here."

I'm about to say something to him when the door opens. "We have incoming," Amelia says. "He is fit to be tied. Chelsea went outside to see if she can calm him." She closes the door behind her.

Mayson shakes his head. "Gotta admit," he says, getting up. "Took him longer than I thought. I'm going to go and save my woman." He takes a step down. "You're going to be okay, Willow," he says softly and then turns. "No matter what, you have me in your corner. We may not be joined by blood, but our bond goes deeper than that."

He turns and walks down the step and around the house. I sit here looking at the sun. My head goes around and around in circles when I see him walking to me. "Hey," he says. Stopping in front of me, he blocks the sun. I look at him, seeing the anguish on his face. "I thought you left," he whispers, shaking his head. "I'm sorry about before."

"It's okay," I say. "I'm sorry for taking off and not leaving a note." I look down.

He comes to me and squats down on the stair in front of me. "No, I'm the one who shouldn't have pushed you," he says. "I'm so, so sorry," he says and takes me in his arms. His smell is all around me. "I was so scared you had left," he says softly, and I just breathe in his smell. It's a scent I didn't even know I was used to. I also didn't realize that with his arms around me, I felt a certain peace I couldn't explain. In his arms, I also knew that everything would be okay.

"Okay, you two, come and eat," Amelia says, opening the back door. "Breakfast is on the table."

She closes back the door, and he lets me go and holds out his hand for me. "Hungry?" he asks, and I just nod.

I reach my hand out to his as I get up, and I let him lead me inside, where I sit down at the table, and I smile. But I still look around, catching Mayson staring at me. He just smiles back at me and leans over to me. "Feels good, doesn't it?" I don't have to answer him because my cheeks hurt from the smile on my face.

Breakfast is so good, and when we leave there, we go back to the barn, where I feed the girls and apologize to Hope. When I go home that night, I walk to the bedroom and don't unpack my bag, but I do put it away under my bed. I take a shower, and for the first time ever, I slip shorts on and then a sweater. I walk out to the couch and see that he's lying on the couch watching television. He looks over, and his mouth opens when he sees me wearing the shorts.

"I know that you bought all those clothes," I say, pointing at the bedroom. "And I know that I probably can't afford all of them." I stop talking, and he sits up, and I hold up my hand. "But I want to pay you back something for them."

"Willow," he says my name.

"I also can't pay you all in one shot," I say. "And I know that you don't want the money. I know you don't need the money. But I need to do this. I need to pay you." I point at my chest.

"Okay," he says softly. "How much do you want to pay me?"

"I have no idea," I say. "I didn't count all of the articles."

"Five hundred." He gives me an amount. "Give me five hundred, and you can have all of those clothes."

"Can I do that in five installments?" I ask.

"Yes," he says, and I smile.

"Perfect," I say, folding my hands into each other. "And thank you."

"You never have to thank me, Willow," he says my name softly. "Not ever."

I nod at him, and all I want to do is sit with him on the couch, but I don't want to intrude, so I turn around and take a step forward. "Willow." I turn back around. "Want to sit and watch a movie with me?" I can't even hide the smile that comes over me.

"Okay," I say softly and walk over to one of the couches and tuck my feet under me.

"What kind of movie do you like watching?" he asks, and I just shrug.

"It's safe to say that I'm not up to date with movies, so anything is fine. As long as it's not scary," I say, and all he does is nod, and for the first time ever, I fall asleep while watching a movie with a smile on my face.

Twenty-Seven

QUINN

"What does one expect at a county fair?" Willow asks me from the passenger side of the truck. For the past two weeks, we have been inseparable, and I haven't been this calm in my whole life. It's like she brings out the good person in me.

We wake up in the morning and watch the sun rise while we ride our horses. I haven't told her yet, but Hope is her horse. Even if I didn't want to give her Hope. Hope has chosen her. She refuses to let anyone near her, except Willow. We've taken the routine of going home and cooking together, something that she actually enjoys doing. Most of the time, we have to throw out the food, but the times that it does turn out, it's really good. My favorite time of the day is when we sit on the swing outside after dinner. We don't say a word to each other, but with my arm around her shoulders, we watch another day slip away from us. She sleeps under the covers when I check on her. She smiles more, she laughs all day long, and for just one second every single day, I close my eyes to listen to the sound of her talking or laughing.

"There are rides that we can go on," I start to say. "Food, games, and sometimes even music."

"Is everyone going to be there?" she asks, and I laugh. She's been to two Sunday lunches, and each time, she's come home exhausted from remembering everyone's name.

"You will definitely see some familiar faces," I say, turning into the parking lot and seeing that it's already full. "But Grandma and Grandpa won't be here."

"Aww," she says, looking over at me. "That's too bad." My grandparents love everyone. It's in their nature, but to see Willow just open up to them is something I will never get used to. She probably doesn't even realize she's doing it. There is just something about my grandmother that leads everyone to tell her everything.

I park the truck and get out, walking around and seeing her get out of the truck. Ever since she said she would pay me for the clothes, she's been wearing new stuff. Not every day, but at least once a week, she wears a new shirt or new jeans. Just like today, she's wearing pink shorts for the first time ever. Showing off her tanned, toned legs has my cock feeling like it is being throttled, with a black and white striped tight shirt showing off how tiny she is. White Converse are on her feet, with her hair blowing loose in the wind.

"Ready?" I say, putting my hand on her back. We walk toward the noise, and once we get close, I look over to see her eyes light up. I see the Ferris wheel going around and hear people laughing close by. I look over and see a couple of kids running around with balloons in their hands.

"Oh my gosh," she says and looks over at me. "It's like in the books." She turns in a circle as she takes in the rides. "Oh, you can win a stuffy." Her face lights up then she frowns and looks at me. "You told me not to bring money."

Already, I let her pay me back a hundred dollars a week for her clothes. There was no fucking way I was going to let her bring money here. "I already paid," I say. "I bought tickets from Harlow." I look at her and pull out the two hundred dollars' worth of tickets I bought. "It was for her school." She just looks at me. "It was for her graduating class."

"Why do I feel like that is just an excuse?" She looks at me, and I'm saved when I hear someone call my name. I turn and look over to see Gabriel running toward us.

I squat down and grab him up in my arms, looking over at Ethan, who walks beside Emily with his daughter on her shoulders. "I smell food," I say, kissing Gabriel's cheek.

"He just inhaled a whole funnel cake," Emily says as she smiles and goes to hug Willow. Ethan looks at her and nods. We spend a couple of minutes talking before Gabriel squirms out of my arms and asks to go play a game.

"Where do you want to go?" I ask, and she just shrugs.

"Let's just walk around," she says, so I walk beside her. Our hands are grazing each other as we walk. My pinky is holding hers longer and longer each time, until I just take the jump and slip my hand into hers. She looks down at our hands and then looks up at me and smiles. If we weren't in the middle of a fucking zoo, I would ask her if I could kiss her. I would push her hair behind her ear and beg to taste her.

"Oh, look." She points at a shooting game. "You think you can win?" she asks, and I just side-eye her. "Should I ask Chelsea when we see her?"

"Very funny," I say, pulling her toward the game. Her laughter fills my soul as I zigzag through the people. "Okay," I say when I get up to the wooden table. Seven barrels are all the way in the back, and there are targets all over the place. There are circles and squares and a couple of five-star sheets.

"What are we going for?" the man behind the wooden table asks.

"What are the choices?" Willow asks the man.

"We have the small one for one shot." He points at the

small stuffed animals that are in a bin. "The middle one, you have to get three shots." He points at the regular one. "And the top." He points at the big stuffed animals hanging on the wall. "That you have to get five star targets."

"Let's do the five," I say, putting money down on the table. He smirks at me and brings me an old gun, putting pellets in there. "Good luck," he says to me, and I want to wipe the smirk off his face as I turn to look at Willow.

"Which one did you want?" I ask her, and she points at a stuffed dog. I assumed she would go for the teddy bear.

I hold up the gun and aim at one of the stars, shooting it in the middle of the white paper. "You can't shoot at the same star."

I look over at him and find the second one I want next. I take the next shot and hit it right in the middle. I snap the third one without thinking twice and also the fourth one. The fifth, though, is a tough one. It's between two other sheets. If I move just a touch, I'll hit the circle. "Um, Quinn." I hear Willow's voice, and I turn to watch as she comes over. "It's okay if you don't win it. We still get the middle one."

She smiles. I don't care how many fucking times it takes; I will have to win her that fucking dog. I get back into the zone and take the last shot I have. It whizzes right into the middle of the star, and I hear Willow yell with glee.

I look over and see her with the biggest smile I've ever seen on her face. It radiates through her. She jumps up and down, clapping her hands. "Good shot," the guy says, walking over to the dog and handing it over the wooden desk to her. "Here you go."

"Oh my goodness," she says, taking it in her hands, and I would have given everything I had to see that look in her eye. I put the gun down and turn toward her.

I smile at her, and she comes to stand in front of me with the dog in her arms. "You got me a dog." She looks down at the dog and then up at me, her eyes glistening with tears, but not sad tears. These are happy tears. I know this because the smile on her face is so big it almost reaches her ears. "You got me a dog," she says again, looking at the dog and then looking at me.

She inches closer until we're standing almost chest to chest. "No one has ever gotten me anything," she says, and all the noise in the background fades away from us. It's like we are the only two people here. My hand comes up to her cheek. I hold her face in my hand, my thumb on her chin, and we both move at the same time. Both of us move toward each other, and here in the middle of the county fair, I finally get what I've wished for. She says my name, "Quinn," right before my lips touch hers.

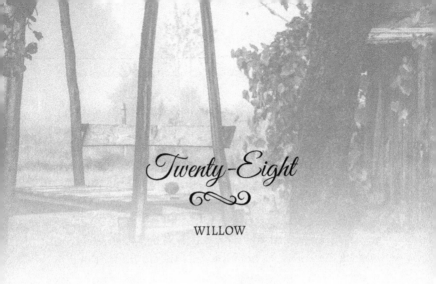

Twenty-Eight

WILLOW

"Quinn," I whisper his name, the sound of laughter and ringing bells fades off into the distance, and it's just him and me. His hand is on my cheek, my eyes on his as I move my lips closer to his.

I hold my breath for fear that he pulls away from me. I have never ever wanted to be kissed in my life, except when I'm around Quinn. I dream about what it would be like to kiss his hand. I dream about what it would feel like to lie on the couch with him. I dream about what it's like to be loved by him. My breath hitches right before his lips touch mine. I want to keep my eyes open to watch it all. I want to keep my eyes open to make sure that I'm not dreaming. But my eyes close slowly as I take in the taste of him. His tongue slips into my mouth, and I fall into him, holding the stuffed dog in one hand, my other hand on his chest. He wraps a hand around my waist, pulling me closer to him. Our tongues slide with each other, and then he slowly lets me go. My eyes flutter open to see his staring at me. "Do you want to get out of here?" he says, and all I can do is nod. "We can stay if you want."

"I want to go." My finger taps his chest as he smiles at me, leaning in again.

He kisses me softly again, stepping away from me, letting my hand fall from his warm chest. He slips his hand into mine as we walk out of the fair. Since the beginning, every single time he's held my hand, I've felt safe. But with our fingers intertwined, I know I have never felt this much peace in my life.

When we got here, it was almost as if I was in a movie. You know the movies that you wish you lived in. When we get to the truck, he opens the door for me. I step in front of him to get into the truck, looking up at him. "Thank you," I say again. "For making this the best day ever." I look down, and when I look up, he is over me, kissing me again. But this time, the kiss is not as soft as before. The need to get him even closer to me kicks into me as I arch my back so I can get closer to him.

Again, he is the one to stop the kiss, and I wonder if I'm doing it wrong. "We have to get out of here before I pull you into the back, and we spend all night here." I look down, trying to hide the fact that my cheeks are burning. I step into the truck and watch as he closes the door.

He gets into the truck, and I turn to look at him when he pulls out of the parking lot. The number of cars has almost doubled since we got here, yet all I saw was Quinn. All I ever see is Quinn. The ride back to his house is quiet. My head goes around and around with things I want to tell him. Things he needs to know. Things I want to share with him.

"I've kissed one guy my whole life," I say, and he looks over at me. "When I turned sixteen." He doesn't say anything knowing that I'm not finished. "I kissed him so I could control who I kissed. It was the only thing I got to choose in my life." I shake my head, thinking about it. "I wasted my first kiss." I look at him. "I didn't want to kiss him. But I did anyway. But you, Quinn," I say his name, and I look up at him. I'm waiting to see him look at me differently. "You, I want to kiss. I want to kiss you all the time. I want to kiss you in the morning when we walk to the barn. I want to kiss you at night when we sit in the swing, and you have your arm around me. I want to kiss you when we sit on the couch, and I watch television," I admit to him, and now that I've let it all out there, I can't stop. "Also, I hate watching television. I'd rather sit with you and just be with you."

"Is that so?" he says, chuckling.

"Um, yeah," I admit. My heart speeds up, and I'm not sure my mouth will listen to my brain when it tells me not to tell him the rest. But my mouth wins out this time. "And I want to hold your hand, but not at the barn because I don't want people to think I'm trying to lure you to my bed." He shakes his head and laughs. "It's not funny, Quinn."

"Okay," he says, looking at me with his back to the door of his truck. "Number one, I don't even know what I put on the television. I put anything that I think will make you stay with me. Number two, I want to wake up with you in my arms every single morning. I want to walk to the barn with you holding your hand. Number three, I don't give a fuck who sees me hold your hand because I don't think you've been paying attention, Willow," he says, and I just look at him. "It's you," he whispers. "It's always been you. It will always be you."

My heart soars in my chest and I can't help the smile that forms. "Now can we go inside and ..."

"And make out?" I ask him, hoping he says yes, I have never been this forward before.

"Oh, we are definitely going to make out," he says, opening his door and I jump out of the truck, grabbing the dog. He is there as soon as I put my feet on the ground and pushes me against the truck. "If you want to stop," he says. "All you have to do is say the word."

"Quinn," I say as he presses his chest into me. "Kiss me," I say and he bends his head. He rubs his nose up and down mine before tilting his head to the side and opening his mouth on mine. I wrap my arm around his neck while my tongue comes out to meet his. He wraps his arm around my waist and picks me up as if I weigh two pounds. My feet don't touch the ground and my lips never leave his as he walks us into the house. Once the door closes behind us, he slowly lowers me to the floor. Once my feet touch the floor, I let go of his lips. Our chests are pounding as I step away from him.

"From the minute that you rescued me, you have never left my side." I start to tell him, and my hand comes up so I can touch his face. My finger trails his chin. "I didn't know what to think having you there." I swallow down the lump in my throat. "But knowing you were there, I felt safe. Which is crazy because I didn't know you and you didn't know me, yet I knew that you wouldn't let anything happen to me."

"I never ever will let anything happen to you, Willow. Ever." His hand comes up and he trails his finger over my face. "Ever."

"I know you won't," I tell him, my heart beating so fast in my chest. Not sure if he is going to turn me away or not. I can't not take the chance with him. "I know you aren't my first kiss." My finger traces his lips. "But I want you to be my first with everything else."

"Willow," he says my name, and I have to wonder if he even wants me. I'm about to take a step back. "Now I don't know what you just thought, but I can tell you that it's probably bullshit." He looks at me. "What did you just think?"

"I, um ..." I try to think of something to say.

"Also, you should know that I know when you're lying," he says, and I roll my eyes. "Your eyes turn a touch darker when you are lying." I stand in front of him shocked he would know this. "And when you're nervous, you tap your finger over and over again. I've watched you for the past two months," he says. "I've watched you build yourself up again. I've watched you work every single day to better yourself. I've watched you fight the demons away. I've watched you silently want things but never ask for it. I've watched you every single day."

"Quinn," I say his name because I don't even know what to say. "I haven't shown anyone the real me, because I don't know who the real me is. But here. With you. It's as real as it gets."

"With you," he says, shaking his head. "The only place in the world I want to be is with you."

I smile up at him, dropping the stuffed dog on the floor and taking his hand in mine. I pull him past the bedroom I sleep in, past the living room, and to the one door I've never stepped inside. "I've thought about what your bedroom looks like," I admit to him. "I wondered if you lie in bed thinking of me." My hand goes out to his chest.

"I haven't slept in the bed since we came home from the hospital," he admits to me. "I was too afraid I wouldn't hear you if you needed me." He pushes the hair behind my ear. "So I stayed on the couch."

I swallow down the lump in my throat. I could have been lying in a pool of blood, bleeding out and my mother would have walked over my body, and this man who owes me nothing wants to give me everything. "Show me your bed, Quinn," I say and he bends down to kiss me and picks me up in his arms.

"This is not how I saw this happening," he says as he walks into his bedroom, and I take it in for the first time. The soft light on from the two lamps on his wooden bedside tables.

His room is massive with the big king-size bed in the

middle of the room. The ceiling on top of the bed has pieces of wood on it, leading to a fan. "I wanted to make you dinner and get candles." He walks over to the bed, and I swear it looks even more comfortable than the bed I sleep in, and that bed is a cloud.

He puts me on the bed, and I sink right in. I open my legs, and he stands between them, pushing my hair from my face. "I am going to cherish every single part of your body," he says, and all I can do is watch the way his lips move. He bends, and I tilt my head back as he kisses my lips.

I look up at him. "Show me," I say, taking my shirt and pulling it over my head.

I lie back on his bed, hoping he comes on the bed with me. I watch his hand clench into a fist, the agony all over his face. "Willow, you have no idea what you do to me."

I lift my hips, slipping the shorts over my hips and tossing them aside. "What do I do to you?" I ask, and he throws his head back to look up at the ceiling.

"I'm afraid to hurt you," he admits. "I'm afraid I'm going to push you too hard."

"You won't hurt me." I sit up and reach out for one of his hands. I bring his hand to my lips. "These hands will never hurt me." I kiss his hand. "Piece by piece." I look up at him. "You put me back together again."

His hand comes up and cups my cheek. "You are so beautiful," he says and pushes me back. His body comes over mine, and I can't believe how lucky I am. His mouth claims mine, and this time, the kiss is all tongue. His tongue fights with mine, and I moan when his fingers trail from my chin to my chest. He stops kissing me, our eyes watching his hand, and he stops at the swell of my breast. "Beautiful isn't even a good enough word for you." He slips his hand into the bra, and my nipple waits for his touch. He pushes down the cup of my bra, and his mouth takes my nipple, and if he wasn't on top of me,

I would have jumped up. I feel it all the way to my stomach, and my legs wrap around his hips. He moves to the other nipple, and my head goes back as I take in all the emotions running through me.

He lets go of the nipple and kisses his way down my side, his tongue trailing down to my stomach. My stomach quivers when he gets lower, and all I can do is watch him in a daze. "I've dreamed of this moment," he says, kissing one of my inner thighs. "At night." He kisses the other thigh. "I wonder what you would taste like. I wonder how it would sound if you yelled out my name."

I tremble, waiting for his touch. I tremble, waiting for his next move. "Quinn," I whisper as I watch him slip my panties to the side, and he growls out right before his tongue slips into me.

Twenty-Nine

QUINN

I can't help the growl that comes out of me right before my tongue slides into her folds. This. This right here is what dreams were made of. I close my eyes as I slip my tongue into her.

Then I open them when I feel her hands in my hair. "Quinn." My eyes look up at her as she writhes under my touch. I lick up to her clit and move my tongue side to side, and she arches her back off the bed. If I wasn't holding her down, I think she would have jumped off the bed. "Oh my God," she says, and my tongue plays with her clit. I lick down and then up, wetting her even more, when I slide a finger in her. "Yes," she pants out, and when I suck her clit in and move my finger a couple of times, I feel her getting wetter and wetter. "I ..." She moves her head from side to side. "Oh." Her hips move on their own as she chases her orgasm. My finger moves faster and faster, and then she screams out my name right before she comes on my finger.

Watching her come has to be the sexiest thing I've ever fucking seen. Watching her watch my every single move, my eyes on her while I made her come. It was the most intimate thing I've ever done. I kiss the side of her leg while she lies there. "Are you okay?" I ask, and she shakes her head. I'm so scared I hurt her. My heart stops in my chest.

"I don't know what this feels like," she says. "But it's better than okay."

I laugh, getting up and taking off my shirt. Her eyes are on my body as I kick off my boots and walk to the side table, taking the condoms out. I feel a knot in my stomach when she watches me, and I want her to know that no one has ever been in this bed but her.

I'm about to tell her when she sits up, and I stop moving. I see her hand come up. "Can I touch you?" Her hand goes to the middle of my chest as she places her palm flat over my heart. She gets on her knees and kisses the center of my chest as she trails her tongue down my stomach. "You're sexy," she says, smirking.

"Is that so?" I say, and her hand goes to the button of my jeans.

"Willow," I call her name, and she looks at me, dropping her hand. "I don't know how much I can take," I say, and she tilts her head. "I've been walking around with a hard-on for a solid week and a half."

She shakes her head, and her hand comes back to the zipper, pulling it down. My cock is trying to escape my boxers, and her hands pull the jeans down over my hips. I watch her slip my boxers down and then look at my cock ready for her. She leans forward and takes the tip in her mouth. My eyes close as my head goes back. "Willow," I grumble when she grabs my shaft in her fist. Looking at her, I see her try to swallow my cock, stopping midway, and then coming up again. She twirls her tongue around the head of my cock and then sucks in deeper, and I have to stop it, or I'm going to come in her mouth, and the first time I come, I'm going to be inside her.

She watches me, her cheeks turning pink. "Lie back," I say, taking off my jeans and boxers. "And open your legs for me." She does as I say, and I roll the condom down my cock. "This might hurt," I say, putting my knee into the bed. I take off her panties and see her glistening in the light. A small landing strip is right above. "I'll go slow," I say, and she just nods.

My hands almost shake from nerves as I lean in and rub my cock between her lips. "Tell me if it gets to be too much," I say, slipping in just a bit. The heat of her pussy is all over my cock as I slide in as slow as I can. Her eyes are looking down the whole time as her pussy takes my cock. In no time, my cock is balls deep in her, and I want nothing more than to move out and slam into her. "You okay?"

"Yeah," she pants out, her hips moving side to side.

I put my hands beside her arms, and she tilts her hips back as I pull my cock out of her pussy and slide in again. This time, it slides in easier. My eyes are on her as I slide back out and then in again. "You are so tight," I say between clenched teeth. My cock feels like it's in a vise. I move a touch quicker now, her hips moving with mine. Her juices run down my balls as I fuck her.

The sound of our pants fills the room. "It's happening," she says. "Oh, God, right there," she says as she locks her legs around my hips. "Don't stop," she says, and I want to tell her that I wouldn't be able to stop for all the money in the world. "Quinn," she cries out my name, and I stop moving my cock because at the same time, I come with her.

I wait until her eyes open before I turn her onto her side, carrying her with me. My cock still in her, I push the hair away from her face. "Are you okay?"

She nods her head. "I'm more than okay." She tilts her head back, and I kiss her.

I slide out of her, and I already miss her. "I'll be right

back," I say, walking to the bathroom, and when I look over, she's following me.

I walk into the bathroom, and she stops at the doorway. "Oh my God," she says, looking at my bathroom. This is the only room I really had a say in. I wanted a huge walk-in shower, with a rainfall shower, jets all along the wall. Right next to a big bathtub for two. "Is that a bathtub or a pool?" She comes in, and I see the twinkle in her eye as I walk over to it and turn on the water.

"Want to take a bath with me?" I ask her, and she smiles, shaking her head. She unclips her bra and steps in, and she has the sexiest body, yet she has no idea.

I take off the condom and then walk to the door. "Where are you going?"

"To get more condoms," I say. "You naked in a bubble bath." My cock springs to action as she laughs.

"Hurry back," she says as I walk out of the room, and then she yells, "Or do you want me to start without you?"

Fuck, I love her, I think, and I stop moving. I love her. I look at the bed I just took her on. I take a step, looking down at her clothes mixed with mine. I love her. I sit on the bed as the realization hits me like a race car coming full force toward the checkered flag. I fell in love with her, and I had no idea. I mean, I know I liked her. I knew that I wanted to make sure she was okay, but love. The love part came when I wasn't expecting it to. "Quinn," she calls my name, and I look over to the bathroom. "Are you okay?" I open the drawer and take the condoms out, swallowing down the fear that she will wake up one day and leave. "Did you change your mind?"

I get up and walk over to the bathroom, finding her with her hair tied to the top of her head as she sits in the middle of the tub with the bubbles coming higher and higher. "Get in here," she says, and I slip into the tub with her, and I make love to her.

-~-

The sound of the alarm makes me stir as I lean backward and shut it off. "What time is it?" I hear from beside me and bring her into my arms.

"Four thirty," I say, kissing her naked shoulder.

"Why so early?" she asks, and I laugh.

"We've been late to the barn for the last two weeks," I say. "So I figured if we woke up early, we could take our time instead of rushing."

She turns in my arms. "I like that idea a lot." She slips her arms around my neck.

The past two weeks have been a dream come true. The day after we walked out of my bedroom with Willow wearing one of my shirts is the day Amelia decided she needed to go home. So it was just the two of us, and we couldn't keep our hands off each other. We would hold hands walking into the barn, and that is where it stopped. Until we came home, then all bets were off. I couldn't keep my hands off her, and luckily for me, she wanted me just as much as I wanted her. We've had sex on every single surface that we could. Her body lighting up for me, and she was good at taking what she wanted. There were times I woke up to her mouth around my cock, and then she would slide down my cock.

"How do you want it?" I ask. I always ask her.

"I want to ride you," she says, and I turn to grab a condom, and she grabs it from me. "I need you now," she says, and out of all the layers of Willow, this has to be my second favorite. She tears the wrapper with her teeth and then rolls it down my cock, and I have enough time to hold my cock up before she slides down it. She leans forward, grabbing on to the headboard, and I take the opportunity to bite her nipple, and just like I know her, she rides my cock harder.

"I was dreaming," she says, using her legs to move up and down, one hand letting go of the headboard as she leans backward. "Of this when the alarm rang," she says, and I use one hand on her hip and another one to play with her clit. With her nipple in my mouth and my finger on her clit, it is no time before she comes all over my cock. I wait for her to stop before I take over.

I take her from behind as she screams out my name over and over again. Then I carry her to the shower where I wake her up with my mouth, and she returns the favor by taking my cock into her mouth. I leave her in the shower as she finally washes her hair. I look over at her, seeing that her body has filled out even more, and I fucking love every inch of her. I also have tasted every single inch just like I promised her I would.

"I forgot my panties," she says. "Can you go and get me a pair?"

I shake my head. "This wouldn't happen if you would move your stuff into the bedroom." I slip on my boxers and jeans, watching her.

I slip my shirt on. "This wouldn't be an issue if you didn't rip off the panties at night." She puts her hands on her hips, and my cock gets hard again. "If you hurry," she tells me, "we can take care of that." She points at my cock, and I walk out of the room, going to her bedroom. I walk into the room that she hasn't used in two weeks. I walk over to the side table where I know she keeps her panties, and I open the drawer taking a handful. I close the drawer, turning when my foot hits something that is under the bed.

I bend down, lifting up the bed skirt, and see the black bag. Her black bag, my heart speeds up, and my head tells me to leave it alone. But my hand moves before I have a chance to stop it. "Please let it be empty," I tell myself, and when I pull it out, it's fully packed. More packed than when we got home. The panties fall out of my hand.

The bag shakes in my hand, and everything happens at

once. "What is taking you so ..." I hear her voice, and then she stops dead in her tracks when she sees me holding the bag in my hand. I look up, seeing her wrapped in a white plush towel.

"What is this?" I ask, and she takes a step forward. "It's full."

I suddenly feel like I'm going to be sick. I shake my head. I know I should take a step back. I know that I should give her the benefit of the doubt. I know all of that, but what I also know is that my heart is broken. It's breaking, and I know deep down inside she was always going to break it. "You will never be at ease, will you?"

"Quinn," she says my name as tears run down her face, and I look at her, this woman who I love with every single part of my being. "It's not—"

"It's not what, Willow?" My own tears fall. "It's not what I think? Because it's pretty much your bag packed, ready for you to leave." The realization hits me like a freight train going a hundred and fifty miles per hour.

"I want to," she says, and I put the bag on the bed. "I just didn't know."

"You didn't know what, Willow? If you wanted to stay," I finish for her, "you would have unpacked the bag." I look at her, my heart shattered in my chest, and I am having trouble breathing. "I can't do this." I walk away from her toward the door and look back at her. Her body is shaking with tears. "I can't be that person who forces you to stay. I will never force you to do something you don't want to do." I look down. "Even if it kills me."

I walk out of the bedroom and straight to the door. My feet get heavier and heavier by the time I reach my truck. "I love you," I say, taking one look back at the window that I know she's in. "But it's not good enough."

Thirty

WILLOW

I stand by the window with tears streaming down my face watching him drive away from me.

His words play over and over again in my head. "I will never force you to do something you don't want to do. Even if it kills me."

I walk back over to the bed, sitting on it right next to the black bag. The black bag that I've had since I was seven. The black bag that I packed when I had to leave the only house I've ever known. Then I packed it every single time we moved, which I lost count at. It was finally the only thing in my life I cared about. It was my lifeline. And it just ruined the best thing I've ever had.

Every single day I fall more in love with this town. From the people who smile at me when I walk into the diner. To the people who come and say hello to me at the barbecue on Sundays. It's like I've been here my whole life. Standing with him in this room and watching him, I know without a shadow of a doubt that this is where I want to be. And he is who I want to be with.

Every single day I fall more and more in love with Quinn.

It happened without me even knowing what was happening since I have never loved anyone in my whole life. I want to be here with him.

I take the black bag and open it to find the clothes I put inside there the week after I arrived at the house. Three pairs of jeans, five shirts, five pairs of panties, and three bras. I place it all on the bed and then reach in and take out the hospital gown. I fold the gown back up and put it back in the bag.

I get dressed in a rush to go and find him to tell him that he won't have to ask me to choose because I chose him a long time ago.

Rushing out of the house, I take the golf cart and make my way over to the barn. Walking in, I don't see him, and I look around and see that he hasn't been in yet because the coffee hasn't been started. I walk over to the machine, pressing the button and then turn toward the office.

Seeing it empty, I grab the phone and call Mayson. He answers after one ring. "Hello." After I had that talk with him on his stairs, whatever crazy bond we had was cemented even more.

"Hey," I say softly. "I'm sorry, I didn't know who else to call," I say honestly, and I can hear him walking.

"It's fine. What's the matter?" he says, and I don't know where to start.

"I," I start to say. "Quinn took off, and I don't know where he is."

My voice goes soft now. "I have to find him."

"Where are you?" he asks me, and I hear a car door close from the phone.

"I'm in the barn," I say.

"I'll be there in five minutes, and we can go and look for him," he says.

"Okay," I say and hang up the phone. Never have I had

someone help me and be on my side, and when I see Mayson pull up three minutes later, I wipe the tears from my face.

"This is silly," I say. "Maybe he's back at home."

"He's at the office," he says, and I look at him confused. "He's at the headquarters."

"I don't know what you are talking about," I say.

"Get in, and I'll take you there," he says, and I open the door and get into the truck.

"Thank you," I say softly when he pulls away from the barn. "For coming."

"You would do the same," he says, and I look over at him. "If I needed help, I know that you would come without asking any questions." I think about his words looking out the window. My heart beats faster and faster as we pull up to another barn. This one however, looks different from all of them. I don't know what it is. It could be that it's painted white and a paved parking lot is all around it.

"Where are we?" I ask him when he turns the truck off. I open my door, stepping out, waiting for Mayson.

"This is where all the magic happens," he says, walking to the door and opening it. I follow him in there, and the cold air hits me right away.

We walk into the cool barn and look at the five white desks in front of another wall. Each desk has a computer on it. "What is this place?" I ask Mayson, who just smiles at me.

"We call it Casey's daycare center," he says, walking to a door and putting his finger on the pad. The sound of the door clicking makes Mayson pull it open. "After you," he says, and I walk ahead of him and take two steps into the room before I stop.

The whole back wall is filled with five big screens side by side. Five desks are on each side of the room with full computers on them. "Oh my God," I say, looking around. "This looks like the headquarters to the FBI."

Mayson laughs beside me. "The FBI wishes they had this system." He walks in, and I follow him to the front of the room. My eyes are focused on the screens in front of me when we come to this big square table that sits in front of the big screens. There are screens built into the desk, and it's all touchscreen. A yellow pad sits on the digital desk. "Let me go find Quinn," Mayson says to me, and he turns to walk out of the room.

My legs walk toward the digital desk as I look down and see that someone was trying to do something. I look down at the paper seeing all this script on it.

I look down at the screen on the table and see that there is a mistake in the coding in one sentence. My hand moves before I can yell at myself to stop.

My eyes move as fast as my hand, the green cursor blinking the whole time I type. It takes me less than three minutes, and I have the system up and running. I look up at the big screen seeing it, and then I hear a voice behind me. I smile and fold my hands over my chest, seeing what I just did.

The sound of the door clicking has me turning around. My hands start to shake when I see Casey standing there looking at me. His eyes go to me and then the screen. He does it two times before he whispers the three words I wanted no one to know. "It was you?"

Thirty-One

QUINN

I pull open the door to the room when I hear my father talking. "It was you?" I walk into the room and stop moving.

My father is standing by the door that leads outside and in the middle of the room right in front of the big desk. The tears are running down her face as her hands shake. "It was you all along, wasn't it?" He puts down his coffee, and Willow looks at me.

"I'm so, so sorry," she says to me, making my heart speed up in my chest.

"What the fuck is going on?" I shout, putting my hands on my hips, feeling Mayson walk to my side, looking at Willow and then my father.

"It was me," she says, trying to stand tall. "I was the reason that your father found you." She looks over at Mayson. "He asked me to see if I could find you. He said that you were his long-lost child." Her voice quivers. "That was when we first met. I found your name change a week later. I found you two days later, but I never told him. I pretended I couldn't find you." Her hands shake, and I want to walk over to her and put my hand around her, but I know she won't want me. I know she doesn't want me. "I never meant for any of this to happen. Never."

"The surveillance feed," my father says, looking at her.

"I hacked your firewall and replayed a loop of when the room was empty," she admits. "But I left a trail." She taps her hand on her leg, "I made the video jump at the end of the loop. I was hoping that you would see it." She uses the same finger she was tapping on her leg to wipe the tear away when it escapes from her eye. "I was hoping that anyone watching the feed would know it was a recording. I never ever wanted anyone to get hurt," she says and looks over at Mayson. "Through all this I just wanted it to end. I wanted you to find him, find us and end it."

"You had no choice," Mayson says. "I can't even imagine what he did to make you do it."

"Behind the computer I could be someone else," she start to tell us. "It made me be invisible. It was just for fun at first but." Willow looks down, and you can tell she has a hard time swallowing. "The minute he found out how good I was is the minute my life really became hell. He made me do things I hated doing. To the point where I never wanted to look at another computer again." She looks down, avoiding my eyes. She's avoided me ever since I walked into the room. She looks up at me. "I'll be out of the house in an hour," she says and then looks at Mayson. "I am so, so sorry for all the hurt and pain I caused you this whole time." She looks at my father. "You had one extra space in the third row, and then in the fifth row, you needed a semicolon." He just looks at her, and she makes a beeline for the door.

"Can someone please tell me what the fuck just happened?" I look at my father and at Mayson.

"She just confirmed to you that she is too good for you," Mayson says. "That woman lived through a hell that we will never know." He laughs. "And trust me, I know because I knew the type of person my father was. But her having that gift, he must have used her like a toy." I look at my father, who is smirking as he looks at the screens.

"You know that I work with some of the best hackers there are," he says. "And you know that I'm the best." He comes over to look at the script on his paper. "But what she did, we've been trying to do for four weeks."

"So what, she's this computer genius," I say. "She's the reason that Chelsea got taken," I point out to Mayson.

"And the reason you found her almost dead is because she said no more," Mayson points out. "Now, if you'll excuse me, I'm going to go and make sure she's okay." He runs out of the room, and I just stand here. I walk over to a chair and sit down. My head is spinning with all this information.

"What the fuck are you doing?" My father looks at me. "Why are you not going after her?"

I rub my hands on my face. "She doesn't want me," I say. "I'm not good enough for her."

I'm waiting for him to tell me otherwise. I'm waiting for him to give me advice, but instead, he looks at me and laughs. "Don't be an idiot." He shakes his head. "If Willow didn't want to be here, she wouldn't be here. All she needed was to take your computer, and she would have had a new ID and a brand-new credit card. She needed five minutes, and she would have everything she needed, but she didn't." He comes to me and slaps my shoulder. "If you let her leave, you will regret it for the rest of your life."

"What if this town is not enough for her." I look at him. "I mean, clearly"—I point at the computer screen—"she's brilliant."

"You don't love her," my father says and turns to walk away, and I jump up. "Because if you love her, the thought of her leaving would cut you off at the knees. So maybe it's better you let her go." He walks to his coffee. "Besides, a woman like that deserves someone who would die for her."

"The thought of not being with her crushes my chest so much I don't think I can breathe," I say, and he looks at me.

"Son," he says. "You're wasting time. Go and get your woman. Jesus." He shakes his head, and I run out of the barn toward my truck.

I make it home in record time, running up the stairs, calling her name when I walk into the house. "Willow," I call her name and rush to her bedroom. I stop in the middle of the room when I see the clothes on the bed. I walk toward it and stop breathing when I see the paychecks she's collected since she's been here with a note on them.

This should pay for the clothes.

"Motherfucker!" I roar out, turning around and looking for that fucking black bag. I take my phone out and call Mayson.

"She's at the barn," he says when he answers. "I promised her ten minutes, and then I would drive her wherever she wanted to go," he hisses out. "Don't make me break my promise to her."

I rush out of the house and take the golf cart, my foot pressed all the way down. I pull up to the barn and see Mayson standing outside his truck, waiting for her. He looks at me and motions with his chin toward the barn, and I walk in, knowing exactly where she is going to be.

I walk slowly down the cement walkway and hear her soft voice. "I'm sorry I have to go, Hope." She sniffles, and my heart breaks. "I will never forget you, sweet girl." I look into the stall and see her with her arms around Hope's neck. "You were one of the things I've loved most about this place," she says softly as I watch her. "You are going to help so many people, my beautiful Hope. You are gentle and kind, and anyone would be happy to have you."

She must sense I'm staring at her because Willow looks up. I can see the anguish on her face. "I was just leaving," she says and bends her head to walk out of the stall. She stops in front of me. "You don't have to forgive me," she says, standing there in front of me. "Because I will never forgive myself. But you have to know that I'm sorry for everything." She bends her head and takes two steps.

"Was everything we shared a lie?" I ask her, and she stops walking. "Turn around and look at me." She doesn't move, but her shoulders shake. I walk to her and put my arms around her. "I love you, Willow," I say finally. "Every single part of you was made for me."

"You don't mean that," she says in my arms. "You can't mean that. Who would love someone like me? I'm a liar." Her whole body shakes, and I turn her in my arms.

"We are not doing this here," I say. "We are going to do this at home." She looks up at me. "Will you come home with me?" I ask her, but the reality is that even if she says no, I'm going to drag her back to the house to listen to me.

"What's the point?" she says, looking at me. "It won't change anything." My heart hammers in my chest. "There is nothing more that needs to be said."

"There are things I need to say. Things that you need to hear," I say, and she steps out of my arms. "Please," I say, and she looks down.

"Mayson is waiting for me," she says.

"Give me five minutes, and if you still want to go, I will drive you wherever you want to go." The lie tastes like acid in my throat.

I turn and walk out of the barn, seeing Mayson still there standing by the truck. He pushes off when he sees me. "I've got her," I say, and he ignores me and looks over my shoulder.

"You going to be okay?" he asks, and she looks at him. He

walks to her and takes a phone out of his pocket. "If you need me, call Chelsea and I'll be right there."

I glare at him when he walks past me to his truck. I take a deep inhale and then walk to her. "The golf cart is over there." I point behind her, and she turns and walks toward it. She sits far away from me, and I hate it. My hands grip the steering wheel so tight I'm surprised it doesn't break off.

I park the golf cart and walk into the house with her following me instead of holding her hand. I turn once I'm in the living room and look at her. "I don't know where you are going to be comfortable doing this." I look at her and see that she is wiping away tears.

"There is nowhere to do this," she says. "Everything has been said. Just let me leave and—" I hold up my hand so she stops talking.

"You think I'd let you leave?" I ask, the next word coming out in a whisper. "Never."

"Quinn, please," she says, her voice cracking.

"I may have been mad," I say. "And stupid for leaving you. But you have to understand that I've never done this before." She wrings her hands together, and my heart feels like someone just kicked it. "I've never been in love before." She gasps out. "You have to know that's how I feel." I walk to her now, my feet not stopping until I'm in front of her. "I will fight for you." My hand comes up and pushes her hair away from her face. "I will fight with you." A sob rips through her. "And I will fight to be with you."

"Quinn," she says, her voice breaking, and I need her to see me. I need her to look me in the eyes.

"You are everything," I say, and I don't even wait for her to say anything before I press my lips to hers.

Thirty-Two

WILLOW

His lips press against mine, and it's a good thing he's holding me because I might have fallen to the floor. I take his kiss and then push away from him.

"You don't mean that," I say, holding on to the couch as my knees shake. "You can't mean that."

"I mean every single word," he says, looking at me. "Every single fucking word."

"But the things I've done," I say, shaking my head. When his father caught me, I knew that my secret would be exposed, the secret that I hoped would never come out. I stood there in front of them and told them that I helped make all of this happen. I stood there, hoping and praying that they wouldn't look at me like I was the monster I was.

"You have done nothing," he says, and I shake my head. "Listen to me and listen to me good." I look at him, putting my hand in front of my mouth right before I sob out. "You did what you needed to do to survive."

"But," I start to say. "But."

"Do you want to stay here?" he asks, and my stomach shoots up to my heart.

"Before all of this," I say the truth because he deserves to know the truth. He needs to know no matter what the future holds, I need to tell him. "Before all of this happened," I start again, shaking the nerves from my hands. "I decided that I was going to tell you that I chose you," I say, my heart feeling the pressure in my chest. "I had picked you. This is where I wanted to be. You are who I wanted to be with. I don't know what love is. I have never felt it before. But just the thought of not being with you. Just the thought of not seeing you every single day, it was a feeling I've never felt before. I was so scared." I swallow. "So scared that one day you would wake up and see that I wasn't worthy of you."

"I'm the one that isn't worthy of you," he says. "I'm the one who left you instead of fighting for you. But when I saw that bag. I had this dread that washed over me that you would leave me, and the thought was too much to bear. I just couldn't." His hands go back to my face. "I can't picture life without you."

The tears roll down my cheeks and over his hands. "That is why I came looking for you," I say. "To tell you that I don't want to leave and that I was going to throw the bag out." I put my hands on his wrists. "But then."

"You don't have to relive it," he says, kissing me softly.

"If I'm going to stay here," I say. "I have to come clean with Chelsea. I don't want to keep this from her." I look into his beautiful blue eyes. "Will you come with me to tell her?"

"I'll go to the end of the earth for you," he says. "Do you want to go now?"

"I do," I say. "I want to go and speak with your dad also."

He looks at me. "You don't have to do all of this today."

"You're wrong. I do. For me and for them," I say, and he nods his head. He holds my hand walking out of the house, as we make our way over to their house. I look out the window as I try to think about what I'm going to tell Chelsea. I know I told Quinn I couldn't live without him, but I know that I can't come between his family. I won't.

We pull up to the house, and he kisses my lips. "No matter what happens, we will get through this," he says, and I know that I have no right to feel sorry for myself. I have no right to feel anything.

He holds my hand, and when Chelsea answers the door, her smile quickly fades when she sees me, and my heart sinks. She knows is the only thing that goes through my mind. "Come in," she says and quickly puts her arms around my shoulders. "Is everything okay? What happened?"

"Um," I start to say, but I stop when Mayson comes into the room. He looks at me and then at Quinn.

"I was wondering if I can have a couple of minutes of your time?" I look at Chelsea and then turn back to look at Mayson. "There are things I need to tell you."

"Of course," Chelsea says as we walk into the house. I sit on the couch with Quinn beside me. Both of my hands are holding one of his. Mayson sits next to Chelsea. "What is going on?" She looks at everyone and then back at me. "I'm getting scared."

"I have a confession to make," I say. "And I want you to know that I never ever wanted anything to happen to you." I look down at my hands and then up at her. "It was me," I say. "I'm the reason he was able to kidnap you."

"It was not you," Mayson says. "It was not you."

"Oh, Willow," Chelsea says, getting up and coming over to my side. "Mayson told me the story, and you have to know I would never blame you. You were a victim, just like everyone else. The only one responsible for this is Benjamin and Benjamin alone."

"But." I shake my head. "But I didn't stop him."

"He would have found a way to get to me regardless if you didn't help him. He was a sick man and he is rotting in hell,"

Chelsea tells me. "Now this man has had enough of my tears. He's had enough of your tears and we know that he's had enough of Mayson's tears."

"I don't know what to say," I answer honestly. "I've never had this kind of support before."

"Well," Chelsea says, laughing while wiping away her tears. "I'd get used to it. You're one of us now." She puts her arm around me again and pulls me to her.

We leave here with me promising that I won't blame myself. I get into the truck, knowing I have another big stop to make. My hands shake the whole time we walk back into the barn. "It's going to be okay."

"I really hope so," I say, not sure at this moment. He pulls open the door, and I see Casey sitting behind a big wooden desk with five computer screens in front of him. He looks up and sees Quinn and then me. He gets up, and I'm expecting him to kick me out of his office. I'm expecting him to tell me not to step foot in here again.

"Well, I can see you took your head out of your ass," he tells Quinn, coming around the desk and smiling at me. "Willow, it's good to see you again."

"Um," I say, confused by his whole demeanor.

"I'm happy you came by," he says, grabbing me in a hug, and I just look at Quinn. He lets me go and leans back, folding his arms over his chest. "I'm assuming you aren't leaving town."

"I," I start to say when Quinn says, "She's staying."

"Good, I want to be the first one to offer you a job," he says, and I open my mouth.

"Now, hold on just a minute," Quinn says. "She has a job."

Casey laughs and looks at me. "It can be part time, but I think that your skills can help us out."

"I don't know what to say," I answer honestly, looking at Casey and then at Quinn. "I didn't ever think ..."

"Why don't you come by on Monday and we can see what we can do?" Casey tells me, and all I can do is nod. Quinn takes me in his arms 'cause he knows I'm two seconds away from sobbing and blubbering in his father's office.

"These are happy tears," I tell Quinn and then look at Casey. "I've never had happy tears before."

"I'm taking her home," Quinn says. "And we aren't coming out for the next two days," he says, and I look down, feeling my cheeks heat.

Quinn puts me in the truck and then looks at me. "We just had our first-ever fight, so we have to make sure we get the making-up part perfect."

"Such a perfectionist." I shake my head, looking at him, and I don't know what I did to be this lucky.

Thirty-Three

QUINN

"Are you almost ready?" I look over at Willow as she stares at her clothes hanging in my closet. Well, our closet.

"Is this new?" She takes the shirt down off the rack and turns to me. "Like, did you buy this for me?"

I avoid her eyes and look away. "I don't think so."

"Quinn?" she calls my name, and I look over at her while I put on my T-shirt. "This is new, isn't it? I'm not dreaming up things."

"Okay, it could be new," I say, shrugging. "My mother brought over some things she bought for you and ..." She opens her mouth. "And I hung them up."

"What?" she asks, shocked as she looks back at the racks. She has more clothes than she knows what to do with. She can go a full year, I think, without washing anything and still be okay. It's my mother's way of showing her how much she loves her. "When?"

"I don't know, a couple of weeks ago," I say the truth. "Or a couple of days ago."

"Well, which is it?" she asks, and I walk to her and take her face in my hands. It's been two months since she has officially decided to stay. Two months since she officially moved into my bedroom. Two months since she officially had not one but two jobs. Two months since she hung up the empty black bag in the closet.

"It could be both," I say and bend down to kiss her. "Now, if you don't hurry, we're going to be later again." I slip my tongue into her mouth this time. "I'm not going to remind you what they thought we were doing." I stop talking when her cheeks go a bright pink, similar to how they turned last Sunday.

"I can't get dressed if you are all over me," she says, and I laugh when she pushes me away from her. She grabs her jean shorts and slips them on her legs, and then puts on the new top she just found, tucking it in the front. She slips on her Converse shoes and then looks at me. "I'm done."

We walk out of the house with her hand in mine, and when we pull up to the barbecue, there are no parking spaces left in the driveway. We park on the street, and again, she reaches for my hand. In the past two months, she's come out of her shell. She kisses me more just because, she holds my hand even in the barn. But the best of all is she laughs and smiles all the time. All. The. Time. And it's glorious.

Every single day, we make dinner side by side, both of us learning. Most of the stuff is edible, while some of it has to be trashed, and then we order pizza. "Do you want to take the horses out tonight?" She looks over at me. "After the barbecue."

"That sounds like a perfect night," I say, and we walk around the side of the house. The backyard is already packed with people.

"Oh, look who it is," Reed says, smirking, with his best friend Christopher beside him. "Only ten minutes late this time," he teases, and I'm about to push his shoulder when I hear my mother's voice.

"Don't hit your brother," she says, and I glare at him as he smirks at me.

"I'm going to head to the barn," Reed says, "and see you all later." He turns and walks toward the barn, where I see some of my cousins on their horses.

"Hey, you two," my mother says when she gets close enough. My father is right behind her as usual. "Willow, you look radiant," she tells her and takes her in a hug.

"Thank you," Willow says, hugging my mother. It has been a slow process with Willow accepting all the love my family has to give, and at times, I feel her holding back because of the fear that it will somehow be ripped away from her. "And thank you for the clothes."

My mother looks at Willow and then at me with her eyes going big as she rolls her lips. "I don't know what you're talking about." She feigns ignorance. "What clothes?"

"Mom," I say.

At the same time, my father says, "Darlin'."

She throws her hands up in the air. "What? Can't I do something nice?"

Willow reaches for my mother's hand, and it surprises even my mother. "It was way too nice of you. I don't need any more clothes."

"One can never have too many clothes," my mother says, looking over at my father. "Right, cowboy?"

He puts his arm around my mother's shoulders. "Right, darlin'." He kisses her lips. "Always right."

I shake my head and feel Willow slip her hand into mine. "Well, for now, how about we stop buying clothes, and one day we can go shopping together?"

My mother gets tears in her eyes and blinks them away. "I would love nothing more." She looks down, and I see her lift her hand to the corner of her eye. "Now go say hello to your grandparents. They were asking for you."

I nod at her and my father, who takes my mother into his arms as we walk away from them. "You really going to go shopping with my mother?" I ask, and she looks up at me.

"She's been asking me, and Chelsea and Amelia said they would come also," Willow says, and we look over toward the cheering and see that Amelia is on her horse with her hands up in the air while Asher just shakes his head.

"I want a rematch!" he yells at her, and she just claps her hands and laughs at him.

"When are you going to get it through your head that you can't beat me at this?" she yells back at him, and he just stares at her. It's a look I don't think I've seen him have before. I stop walking and look over at them, and I'm about to say something to Willow when I hear my grandmother say my name.

"Quinn, honey." I turn my head and see her walking to us, her hair tied in a braid at the side. "I made you two apple pies and some blueberry scones." She looks at Willow. "I also made you blueberry cheesecake."

"You didn't have to do that," Willow says, letting go of my hand to hug my grandmother.

"I have nothing else to do during the day," she says to Willow. "I'm still waiting for you to come and bake with me." Willow looks down shyly. There is no way around it. Willow has captured the love of everyone that met her.

"One day," she says softly. "One day."

"Good. Go get yourself something to eat." She cups Willow's face and smiles at her with all the love she has. It's the way she looks at all of us.

We walk away from my grandmother, and I look over at Willow, who is wiping a tear from her eye. "What's wrong?"

She laughs and blinks away more tears. "Absolutely nothing," she says. "It's just ..." She looks down, and I know what she's saying. "It's a good day." I kiss her lips as we walk up to the line at the tables right behind Amelia, Asher, Mayson, and Chelsea. "Hey, everyone."

"One of these days." I hear Ethan behind us. "We will get here before everyone and be the first in line," he says, and we all laugh, especially Emily, who just shakes her head.

"One can hope," Emily says, and just then, all of our phones go off. I look at Ethan, and he looks at me. I pull my phone out, and the commotion behind me makes me look up as I see my father and uncle running.

I look down and then look up at the black smoke filling the sky. "One of the barns is on fire."

Epilogue One

QUINN

One Year Later

"I forgot something at the barn." I look over at Willow as she wipes down the counter we just ate dinner on.

"Okay." She looks up at me, and she is even more beautiful than the first day I saw her. "Go get it."

I look down, and my heart speeds up nervously. "Do you want to come with me?"

"You're acting weird." She looks at me, and I roll my eyes.

"How am I acting weird?" I ask, folding my arms over my chest, knowing exactly how I'm being weird.

"Well, for one, you didn't attack me when I walked in from work." She tilts her head to the side. She works with my father every single day from one in the afternoon until five. It's the only hours we aren't together, and every time she walks in the door, I spend a good hour making up for the lost time. "And you want me to come with you to the barn instead of 'getting naked.'" She uses her fingers in air quotes.

"Number one, I was cooking when you walked in," I tell her.

"Which is another weird thing because you always wait for me," she says, walking over to me and washing her hands.

"Would you just come with me?" I say. She laughs at me and walks to the front door to get her shoes. I look at her walk away and the picture of us right on the table. There are actually pictures of us everywhere. Us at the barn, us with our horses, us at one of the barbecues. And in every picture, Willow's face is lit up with smiles.

"Okay," she says, walking back, and I take another look at her. She is wearing white jeans and a jean shirt that is loose on her and tucked in. "Let's go."

She slides her hand in mine when we walk out of the house. "We should have everyone over this weekend," she says, looking over at me. "So the pool finally gets used."

"That sounds good," I say, tapping the steering wheel before I tell her that it's already planned. "It's a beautiful night, isn't it."

"It is," she says, and I look down instead of looking over at her. We pull up to the barn, and I look at her. "Do I have enough time to go and say hello to Hope?" she asks, and I just nod at her. She walks into the barn, and the lights are off as I follow her in.

She walks over to the barn and turns on the lights, and instead of the bright lights, only soft lights come on. Lights are hanging all the way down to Hope's stall. She looks up and takes in the lights at the end of the stall in the shape of a heart.

She stops walking and then turns to look at me, finding me right behind her and down on one knee. Her hands go to her mouth, and she sobs out and bends at the waist. "Willow," I say her name softly as she stands there, her whole body shaking. "One year ago today, I took you in my arms," I say, and I see the look on her face as she realizes what the date is. "You barely had a heartbeat, and if truth be told, I would have given you my heart back then. I would have had my heart beat for you even back then. I can't explain to you how or why it happened. The only thing I can tell you is that you were made for me. All of you was made for me. We were made for each other." She shakes, not saying anything, and I take out the black box my father gave me six months ago. "I wanted to get you a ring that was perfect for you," I say. "But my father had other plans." I open the ring. "This ring is the one he gave my mother when he asked her to marry him."

"I can't take your family's ring," she says, putting her hand on her heart.

"Don't you get it?" I say. "It is their way of showing you that you are theirs also," I say. Her legs give out, and I catch her around her waist. "Willow Davis," I say her name again. "Will you be my wife? Will you hold my hand every single day? Will you grow old with me?"

"Are you sure?" She looks at me. "Are you really sure?"

"I haven't been more sure of anything in my whole life," I say.

"Quinn," she says. "From the moment I opened my eyes one year ago, I have never felt so safe. From the moment I felt your hand in mine, I knew that your hands would be the ones to pick me up instead of push me down. I fell in love with you without even knowing what love is." She moves her hand up to my face. "You, Quinn Barnes, made my heart beat with your love." She smiles. "So yes, I'll marry you." She inches her face closer to me, and here in the middle of the barn where she slowly opened up her heart and life to me, I make her mine.

Epilogue Two

WILLOW

Two Years Later

"Well, you have to give her something. She's in pain," Quinn says, putting his hands on his hips.

"I am not in pain," I say from the hospital bed, then I look at the nurse who looks like she is going to kill my husband. "He's just nervous."

"You don't say." She turns, shaking her head, and walks out of the room.

"You are a liar, Willow Barnes," he says. "I saw you flinch."

"It was a contraction," I say. "I'm supposed to flinch."

"Well, they have drugs for that." He runs his hands through his hair.

"Oh, I heard you were back." I look toward the door at Shirley, who walks in smiling. Ever since I left the hospital, I have kept in touch with her. She claps her hands together. "It's the third time in a week."

I roll my lips, trying to hide the laughter. "It's the real deal this time," I tell her.

"Her doctor accidentally broke her water," Quinn says.

214

"Who does that? You need a new doctor." He looks at me, and I shake my head.

"We came as fast as we could," Olivia says, walking into the room with two big bags. "I got the bag for the baby." She holds up the bag she helped me pack a month ago. "And then I threw something in this bag for you."

"Thank you," I say, and she just smiles at me. She has been the mother I have never had. She has accepted me with open arms, and she treats me just like she does her children.

"I have to get back to my floor," Shirley says. "I'll check in later." She then looks at Quinn. "Don't get thrown out of the hospital." She laughs.

"Quinn, go and help your dad with the bags." Olivia looks at him.

"Bags?" He looks at her.

"You think your grandmother isn't going to pack food for after?" She shakes her head. "It's like you don't even know her."

"I'll be right back," he says, kissing my lips. "Don't do anything without me."

"Good God, Quinn," Olivia says. "You are going for five minutes, not five hours." She shoos him out of the room.

I rub my stomach and then look down. "What's wrong?" she says, coming beside me and sitting on the bed. "You had a fake smile ever since I walked in, and if my son was in his right mind, he would have seen it."

I smile shyly at her. "I'm just ..." I start to say, and the tears come regardless of how much I try to fight them back. "I'm scared."

"Oh, honey." She grabs my hand. "It's going to be okay. It might be painful, but you'll forget about it."

I shake my head. "No, not that," I say, and I feel a soft kick. "I don't know how to be a good mother," I admit. "I mean, I've watched you, and I know the kind of mother I want to be." I wipe my cheek. "But what if I don't have it in me?"

"Willow, my mother was not the greatest," she says. "And if you think about it, we had similar experiences with our mothers. Yours always wanted something from you, and mine used me to better herself." I look at her shocked. "And before I moved here, I never thought I would have kids. But then I was around Charlotte, and I saw how she was with Casey and Kallie, and I knew that was the mother I wanted to be." She wipes her own tears. "Ask yourself this ... Would you die for your child?"

"Of course," I answer her. "I haven't even met her, and I know I would trade my life for hers."

"That," she says, "isn't something our mothers would have done. For that, you are already better than her."

"Why is she crying?" Quinn says, dropping the bag at the door and rushing to me. "Are you hurt? I told that nurse that you had pain."

"She's fine," Olivia says. "Everything is going to be fine."

She nods at me, and I smile at her. Six hours later, she is by my side, holding my hand while Quinn holds my other hand. "I love you more than life," he whispers as I give one final push.

Everything happens so suddenly. The doctor places my child on my chest, and I look down. "We have a girl," the doctor says as I sob.

"I love you so much, baby girl," I tell my daughter. "So, so much." The nurse rubs the baby's back, and then she lets out the best sound I've ever heard in my life. Her cry.

I look over at Quinn, who has his head pushed to me. "You did it, Willow," he says with his own tears running down his face.

"No," I say. "We did it."

Also by Natasha Madison

Southern Wedding Series

Mine To Have

Mine To Hold

Mine To Cherish

Mine To Love

The Only One Series

Only One Kiss

Only One Chance

Only One Night

Only One Touch

Only One Regret

Only One Moment

Only One Love

Only One Forever

Southern Series

Southern Chance

Southern Comfort

Southern Storm

Southern Sunrise

Southern Heart

Southern Heat

Southern Secrets

Southern Sunshine

This Is

This Is Crazy

This Is Wild

This Is Love

This Is Forever

Hollywood Royalty

Hollywood Playboy

Hollywood Princess

Hollywood Prince

Something Series

Something So Right

Something So Perfect

Something So Irresistible

Something So Unscripted

Something So BOX SET

Tempt Series

Tempt The Boss

Tempt The Playboy

Tempt The Hookup

Heaven & Hell Series

Hell and Back

Pieces of Heaven

Heaven & Hell Box Set